Jairus' Daughter

Evelyn Weissman

BALBOA.
PRESS

Balboa Press books may be ordered through booksellers or by contacting:

Balboa Press
A Division of Hay House
1663 Liberty Drive
Bloomington, IN 47403
www.balboapresspress.com
1-(877) 407-4847

Because of the dynamic nature of the Internet, any Web addresses or
links contained in this book may have changed since publication and
may no longer be valid. The views expressed in this work are solely those
of the author and do not necessarily reflect the views of the publisher,
and the publisher hereby disclaims any responsibility for them.

ISBN: 978-1-4525-0035-5 (sc)
ISBN: 978-1-4525-0036-2 (e)

The author of this book does not dispense medical advice or prescribe the use
of any technique as a form of treatment for physical, emotional, or medical
problems without the advice of a physician, either directly or indirectly. The
intent of the author is only to offer information of a general nature to help
you in your quest for emotional and spiritual well-being. In the event you use
any of the information in this book for yourself, which is your constitutional
right, the author and the publisher assume no responsibility for your actions.

Printed in the United States of America
Balboa Press rev. date: 10/25/2010

Contents

Introduction

This book was written to answer questions. It is what I call a "fictional autobiography". The material is based on real events and real people but there was so much I didn't know, the majority is a work of fiction.

My children have asked where we came from. Our family is so small; the critical characters are long gone. I have put together a series of stories for my children so they might get an idea of where we came from although they will not get to meet their relatives of my parents' generation.

Others have asked how we became Christians, having been raised in traditional Jewish culture. More than "how", they have asked "why" and this book is my explanation.

Jairus' Daughter is a tale from the Gospels which resonated with me the instant I read it. It is significant in the story of my spiritual search at many levels.

If you are a member of my family, I hope you will get some answers to your questions. If you are a friend, or a curious seeker, I hope this book will give answers as well.

Chapter 1
The Punishment

"I can't live in one of those infernal boxes!" Grandpa said, referring to the apartment houses that lined Ocean Parkway on both sides of the street, far as one could see.

"They are like chicken coops stacked one on top of the other with no room to breathe, to move, to live."

His memory of the shtetl was far distant. The memory of the little houses, the dirt roads, the horses and yes, the chicken coops. It was better there. Better except for the constant threat to one's existence, he supposed.

So now the Rabbi was in America with his family. He brought them over. They waited on the boat to see him in the New World, "Americki". He greeted them at the dock proudly offering apple pie and bananas, symbols of the new life, the new ways. They threw them overboard into the East River and headed home to a crowded tenement.

Years later, he stood with his now grown children and his grandchildren who were (almost) Americans and refused their offer of an apartment nearer their own.

Fiercely clinging to his judgment of the new way of life, he remained transfixed, staring at the tall buildings each of which housed hundreds of people. As the sun began to set above the copper roof of one of the buildings, he recalled another memory, one so distant no one knew of it but he himself and it had been buried so long even he thought it had been gone forever.

He was a young man, a student at a Rabbinical Seminary in Vilna, Lithuania. How he loved to learn! The Rabbis would ask questions and the student would try to answer them. They always fell short. The Rabbis were all so wise. Where did this wisdom come from? Constant study and prayer was their answer. Work and learn. This was what a Jewish man was born to do.

"But where was the origin of this wisdom?" he thought, "Where did it all begin? Someone must have been taught by someone else until one got back to the original teacher. Who was that?"

He drifted into a daydream, the same one that got him into trouble all the time. He thought of Moses and the Patriarchs and the giving of the Law on Mount Sinai. "Did Moses really see God? What did God look like? What did He say? What did His voice sound like? Can anyone actually see God and live?"

"Mordechai! Mordechai!"

He was startled by the sound of the teacher's voice. "Are you daydreaming again? Pay attention to the lesson at hand. Such a shame such a bright student would waste time on such a fruitless occupation."

"Rabbi, you are so wise, where does all wisdom come from?"

"It comes from study and hard work; thinking, not dreaming. Get your mind back in the room and work on today's lessons."

Mordechai was a good student; one of the better ones in fact. The problem was that he asked a lot of questions the Rabbis had difficulty answering. Although he was told not to ask such questions, he couldn't help himself. That was why it was no surprise when the punishment came.

He thought it would be another assignment, one he could polish off in a few hours and have it done. How surprised he was when he was told to pack his things and get ready to take a little trip.

Where he went was a place that caused him to tremble. He had heard about this place in stories told in the town. It was a place that was forbidden to him and to all good Jewish men. Sons of the Covenant would be stricken dead if they ever set foot in there, The Russian Orthodox Church with its onion dome shining in the sun.

He was led into the church by a young man, a student like himself from the "other side". They exchanged pleasantries in Russian, Mordechai trembling and sweating the whole time. "Please don't let me die, or at least don't let me throw up" he thought. There were icons and elaborate crucifixes placed on every available arch and screen. The walls were painted with vivid scenes from the life and death of Christ.

"You won't die just because you walked into this church." The student told him.

"That's what the serpent said to Eve in the garden." Grandpa replied.

"I am a student, like you. We study to be teachers of our faith just as you study yours."

"Thou shalt not make graven images" he said, looking downward to avoid looking at all the graven images surrounding him.

"I have been instructed to welcome you and show you around our church and seminary. You are our honored guest. I am happy to meet one who can read the Holy Scriptures

3

in their original Hebrew language. I have been struggling with this language for the longest time in my lessons. I am not as quick a study as you are reported to be."

"Thank you for your kind words; but I am here for some sort of punishment. I am not such a good student either. I daydream in class and ask too many questions, questions about forbidden things."

"You are here because our Bishop spoke to your Rabbi and asked if he would send one of the better students to visit us and help with our studies of the scriptures in Hebrew. If you can get past the mortal fear you have of this place, you might find yourself assisting us Gentiles with our studies."

"Oh, so that's it!"

He felt a little better about being in that place of idol worship and blasphemy now that he knew the rabbi wasn't damning him to an eternity in hell just because he asked a few questions. He was doing it in order to educate the Gentiles. Perhaps he could be of some help with the Hebrew; but how could he get past the rest?

He agreed to help if the students would understand he was only a biblical translator and biblical scholar and they would require nothing else of him, no friendship, no small talk, no proselytizing of their faith.

He prayed continually that God would protect him from these Heathens for the time he was there. He made a deal with God. If God didn't tell anyone where Mordechai was, he would become and even more devoted student and never , ever again ask another difficult question.

The men on the seminary knew about the Jewish laws. They had gone to great lengths to prepare suitable food for Grandpa although it would never be quite right. They were Gentiles. They touched the food, thereby contaminating it. He ate little at the seminary. He also got very little sleep. Yes, this was a punishment.

One day, after he had been there for several weeks, the priest in charge of the seminary called him into his office.

"The students have been very pleased with the help you have given them in the study of the Hebrew testament. I am pleased myself that you have been able to do this work even though I know you are uneasy in this place.

"Thank you, Sir, Father. Should I call you Father?"

"That is what I am called. Father Gregory."

"Father Gregory, how much longer must I stay here and teach?"

"That is up to you for the most part. I would be honored if you would stay for a long time."

"I must get back to my own seminary."

"Haven't you wondered why no one has come to take you back?"

"I have.'

"They know you are here. They are prepared to let you stay as long as you wish. Are you happy here?"

"I am as happy as I can be under the circumstances."

Father Gregory gave him a knowing smile and began to speak to him in Yiddish.

"Mordechai, my son, I am a Jew like yourself. I know how hard it is for you to understand this but we follow the same religion. We worship the same God, the God of Abraham, Isaac and Jacob."

"How can you say that when you have become a Christian?"

"It is difficult for you to understand this now, my son. I ask the Rabbis from time to time to send promising young scholars from their seminary to help us out. It is the same one I studied at as a young man so they know me. Sometimes there is a student like myself who asks a lot of questions. Some decide to remain here and study to become priests in this church as I did. In this church I found answers to my questions."

"How can you tell me this? Do you really believe all this? Do you believe in the Christian faith?"

"Yes."

"How can you, you are a Jew?"

"Jesus was a Jew."

"Do you believe he was the Moschiach, the chosen one of God?"

"Yes, that's why I am here. Believe me, son, it is the same religion, our religion; our sacred faith."

"It is so different."

" It only seems that way until you know more about it. Think about it."

To say Mordechai was confused was an understatement. He asked if he could talk with Father Gregory a bit more and perhaps read something so he would understand what would influence a Son of the Covenant like Father Gregory to defect to the enemy.

Even more troublesome was the question of why his Rabbi would send students to that defector under the guise of having them help with the Hebrew when Father Gregory could do just as well himself. Was there a conspiracy between his seminary and the Russian church to send the most difficult rabbinical students to the Christians for punishment? Perhaps it was easier to save face this way. If he wouldn't make a good rabbi, maybe he might be eliminated be sending him away to a place where he would never be seen or heard from again. There would be no embarrassment at all. There would be no shame in his not completing his studies. He would simply disappear. Even his own family would consider him dead, once he became a Christian.

He thought and thought about this. He asked Father Gregory even more questions than he had asked his own

Rabbi. He read the Christian Gospels and began to understand what the Christian faith was about. He prayed about it.

When he was ready to give his life to Christ and join Father Gregory's seminary as a student, he had a dream.

He dreamt he was at home. His long deceased grandfather was with him. He was telling his grandfather the most amazing story. He had been tricked into going to the Christian seminary as a teacher of Hebrew so students there might better understand the scriptures in their original language. While he was there, he met Father Gregory, a former rabbinical student who had become a priest in that church. After getting to know Father Gregory, he began to understand why one would want to become a Christian and he was going to join the church himself.

His grandfather stood up and boxed Mordechai's ears. He pulled the boy up by his ears with all his might and threatened him, telling him he was not to do this. His grandfather had made a promise to God when Mordechai was born that the child would become a rabbi and no one was going to stop that promise from being fulfilled.

Mordechai went to Father Gregory the next morning, his ears still ringing from his grandfather's pulling on them in the dream. With tears in his eyes, he explained why he couldn't stay and begged for God's forgiveness for the choice he had to make, choosing not to dishonor his ancestor's promise.

Now, he stood watching the sun setting over the copper roof of the apartment house, recalling the sun on the onion domes of the church in Vilna decades before. He thought of Father Gregory and his own promise for long ago. Where would he be standing now if he had not done what he did that day?

"There but for the grace of God", he thought.

Was this God's grace or was it God's grace he should become a Christian? He never forgot what Father Gregory taught him and never forgot his promise to give his life to Christ.

Was it ever too late?

Chapter 2
The Scapegoat

The teddy bear was wedged between the wall and the back of the radiator. It was covered with dust and it was hot. Who knew how long it had been there?

Sarah retrieved it from its prison and began to throw it around, shouting at it in the unintelligible speech of a one year old. She told it how bad it had been and how it deserved to remain hidden and separated from the other toys.

This was the only toy that never came out, that never was played with; but to be thrown about on the floor and beaten. When she beat the bear, clouds of dust emerged from its brown fur. "Where did this naughty bear come from?" she thought. She couldn't remember a time before the bear. It was always in her room.

Every few days, Sarah would encounter the bear as she played on the floor. Invariably, she would forget it was even in the room until she came upon it once again. She thought, as a child of her age would, that this bear appeared and reappeared by its own will. No amount of rejection or physical abuse kept it from coming back.

When she was done with the bear, she climbed into her crib and began to play with her own feet.

Sarah's crib was in the room where her parents slept. So was the teddy bear although they did not seem to notice it. The other toys were out where they were visible. No one asked about the bear although surely her mother would have encountered it when she cleaned.

Sarah's feet were long and narrow. She was so young that at times she did not recognize them as being part of her body.

On this day she played with her feet as she often did, sucking on her toes to calm herself after a difficult session with the bad teddy bear. On the bottoms of her feet, she noticed some little red spots, blisters, actually. She picked at them with her fingers and then tried to put them in her mouth. They were a curiosity to her but little more than that. She rocked herself to sleep with her toes in her mouth.

That was Sarah's earliest memory.

Sarah was the only child of two older parents who was told she was heaven's gift to them. She was told she was an angel, an answer to prayer for a childless couple who had been married for ten years before her birth.

Sarah, long and slender at birth had dainty long fingers and toes. Surely she would grow up to be an artist or musician. Surely she would fulfill the dreams of her parents whose childhoods were cut short by hard times forcing both of them to leave school and enter the work force at the age of fourteen.

"What do you need that for?" asked Grandma Rivka when Sarah's mother, Esther announced she was pregnant with Sarah. "You need that like a hole in the head."

Perhaps Rivka was right in saying this to Esther. She was her mother after all and Esther was known for being unstable. Her life with Adam was far from ideal. They had married late. He was ill with a heart condition he had acquired in childhood when he had Diphtheria. He was not expected to live to adulthood and now he was thirty nine years old and a father-to-be.

Esther made it her personal campaign to take care of Adam, to care for his high blood pressure by providing him a salt-free diet and making sure he took his Reserpine, a medication that although it did wonders for his blood pressure caused depression as a side effect.

Adam had a family history of depression . The medication made worse what was already there. It was Esther's triumph he had lived for ten years after they had married.

When Esther's sister Lydia had become pregnant out of wedlock, Esther asked Adam if they might keep and raise the baby when it was born and raise it as their own.

"I'm not going to be a father to someone else's bastard!" he screamed. "If I want to have a child I'll have one of my own."

Enter Sarah, floating in the amnion saturated with Esther's borderline personality.

Esther, the borderline, the multiple: Which personality will it be today? No matter which one it was, it had an eating disorder. Guilt and withholding were her primary mechanisms for survival. Since she had no stable personality of her own, she adopted personalities of others at will. When she spoke it was in riddles. At first, they sounded very wise, like parables, until one discovered there was no meaning behind them. They were fragments of thoughts that may have once had wisdom but the wisdom was long ago lost when Esther translated them into magic formulas for magical thinking.

Many years later when Sarah attended college and studied psychology she read about the new experiments on mothering done with monkeys.

One group of monkeys was raised in an environment with a "cloth mother", a dummy made of wire that looked like a female monkey with a baby bottle in its center. The wire dummy was covered with soft terry-cloth so a baby monkey could climb on it and cuddle. The other group was housed with "wire mothers", the same dummy without the terry-cloth covering. All the babies had the same environmental variables. The only difference was the "cloth" and "wire mothers"

Sarah decided her own psychological problems arose from being raised by a human "wire mother".

In order to compensate for the tactile deprivation she experienced as an infant, Sarah used parts of her own body for comfort. This was not unusual behavior for an infant but for her it was a necessity. She rocked herself to sleep, crying almost every night.

When she was a bit older, perhaps two years, she noticed the scars from the blisters she had noticed long before on the bottoms of her feet. She called them to the attention of her mother. "What are they? How did I get them?"

Her mother made up some answer and went to her father, speaking to him in Yiddish saying, "She knows about them. She has seen them. What shall we do?"

Sarah heard the discussion and waited for her answer. She was told that a nurse took care of her for one day after she was brought home from the hospital as a newborn. The nurse burned the bottom of her feet with cigarettes. Her parents then dismissed the nurse after the one day of care,

At the time she was told this, she accepted it.

Years later, she realized her mother had also smoked while caring for her.

Sarah punished the bad teddy bear for he was the reminder of what was bad about her. Her wire mother told her again and again about her intrinsic evil nature, how she was "The Devil Incarnate". Everything about her father that was evil (and there was a lot) was expressed in her. She looked like him and had so many of his negative traits she was destined to grow up to become exactly like him.

As long as the teddy bear stayed behind the radiator, she could sometimes forget about her own worthlessness.

Chapter 3
A Child's Life

Sifting through the jumbled pile of childhood memories of the years before she was able to read or write, Sarah found Tipoo, The Eskimo Boy.

Her mother had borrowed the book from the local library and had read it to Sarah. There were other books in the stack she brought home but Tipoo was the one that Sarah loved.

Tipoo lived in Alaska. In the summertime, his house was a domed structure made of mud and stones with a hole in the center so smoke from the fire inside might exit. The inside of the hut was covered with skins of animals his father caught. His mother and older sisters prepared the skins to hang on the walls. The winter home was an igloo, a structure that fascinated Sarah. The men went hunting in the winter for seals and fished through holes in the ice.

Sarah set up her Eskimo camp under the dining table. Once under there she became Tipoo. Her modeling clay was shaped into fish. She constructed a fishing pole and hook to catch them through a pretend hole in the pretend ice. Once caught, the fish were placed on the radiator cover to cook. They were ready when the clay became shiny and the odor of the hot clay permeated the room. Her summer house was decorated with skins of construction paper. How she loved the time she spent in that place! She made her mother read that book again and again. It was renewed often from the library. Sarah needed to hear the details often to keep up the character of Tipoo.

There were so many visual memories from early childhood;pictures in beloved books, The Golden Bible with its beautiful illustrations of David and Goliath, of Moses and the burning bush, of Ruth and Naomi. She had a book of nursery rhymes. Her favorite pictures in this book were the Musicians of Bremen and of a baker making cakes. The baker was a large man with a jolly smile. He wore a cook's apron and hat and held a mixing bowl and spoon. He was stirring dough that contained flecks of different colors, like a rainbow. When Sarah imagined how that would taste, she thought of her Grandma adding vanilla to her sugar cookies.

The smell of vanilla was like the smell of the benzoin her Daddy used to put in her vaporizer at night. The smell was long buried in her memory to be reawakened when she used it in her surgical residency. What wonderful memories of Daddy and Grandma!

At night when she was a child, Sarah would climb the rope in the center of her bedroom and head for the ceiling where she could watch what was happening in the room below. She often wondered why she was the only one who climbed the rope. "Perhaps", she thought, "the other people were too big and heavy to climb it".

When she told her parents about the rope they were patient in explaining she was only dreaming when she experienced that. "If I were dreaming, why does my head still hurt where I bumped it on the ceiling?"

Sarah had a hard time differentiating her dream world from her waking one for both were so alike. One difference was that in her dreams she had a narrator, the kindly voice of a man who explained the action in the dream much like a narrator in a children's play explains the story to the audience.

In real life, without the narrator, she was on her own. She watched her dreams like she watched cartoons on television. She had not yet seen a movie as she was too young. Television was in black and white back then and the screen was small, only twelve inches in diagonal. She prayed she would be able to see television in color one day. She prayed that her little black and white TV would become a color TV and it did, only once. She and her favorite Aunt Leah were watching a cartoon story. It was "Alice in Wonderland" a story that was new to Sarah. As she watched, she prayed and watched the picture become colored. "Look at that!" she called to Aunt Leah, "The story really is in color!" Leah explained that Sarah only imagined the colors in the picture. "Too bad Leah couldn't see it too." She thought.

One of the more exciting memories she had at that age was when the apartment was painted and redecorated. The two-room apartment was fast becoming too small for the three of them. Sarah was still sleeping in the bedroom with her parents. She needed her own room and they needed theirs. Her parents bought a convertible couch to sleep on in the living room and gave Sarah their maple sleigh bed. How she loved that bed. It became a sleigh that took her on fantasy voyages every night.

Her mother also had a plan to design a kitchen area. She had seen a room divider which could be used as a counter for dining as well as preparing meals. The back side had shelves for storage. Esther wanted one of these for the apartment. It had to be specially built. Sarah and Esther visited the home of a woman who had such a "bar" and they looked at it to see if it was what Esther wanted. The woman gave Sarah a tiny toy chick to play with while the women talked. The chick was made of spun sugar. "You may keep that and eat it if you wish." The woman told Sarah. Sarah kept it as a pet She would never eat anything a pretty as that.

The bar was built and the apartment was painted. The old furniture was moved around or given away and Sarah had her own room. Esther had her kitchen. The dining table Tipoo lived under was moved aside for when company came.

The best thing about having her own room was having her own windows to look out of to watch what was happening on the street below. She could lie on her sleigh bed, look out of the window and dream of trips anywhere her imagination would take her.

She recalled the best day of her life. She was four years old, sitting at her red formica play table. It had been her feeding table when she was younger. She had long since outgrown the central seat which now was folded over as part of the play surface. She had a wooden slatted child's chair drawn up to the table.

On that day a song was playing on the radio, Patsy Cline singing "You Belong To Me". Sarah was playing with her modeling clay. A beam of sunlight streamed in from the window and Sarah was working hard, learning to form letters of the alphabet with the clay. She had a puzzle board of letters that could be removed and used as models for her own clay letters. That was when it clicked! Sarah figured out the key to being able to understand what was written in the books her mother read to her and was beginning to be able to use the letters to make words; her own words, not the ones other people put into the books. She would be going to school soon to learn how to do this. She knew about school as some of her cousins close to her age had already begun to go. Some of the little girls she played with had also started. Her time was coming soon. Her mother had told her so.

One day, not long after that, there was a knock at the door and a mailman delivered a package. It was wrapped in brown paper. The package was for Sarah "For me! For me! What could it be?"

It was a briefcase for school sent from her aunt and uncle. The briefcase was filled with school supplies, pencils, a ruler, a pencil case, crayons and a pair of scissors. These were thing she would need when she would start school in a few weeks.

"A bookcase! Look Mommy, Uncle Sam and Aunt Mae sent me a bookcase for school!"

"That's a briefcase."

"Why would it be called that? You put books in it."

"A bookcase is a piece of furniture like that one over there with books in it. You don't want to carry that to school."

"A briefcase, then, even if it doesn't make any sense."

School was certainly a lot of fun. Sarah went to afternoon kindergarten for her birthday was in July. The schools were so crowded due to the post war baby boom that split sessions were needed to accommodate all the children. Even with the split sessions, there were thirty five children in her class. There were two teachers and lots of children to get to know.

The first day was great. Mother stayed in a little seat on the side of the room with the other mothers as the children got to know each other and the teachers. There were blocks to play with and poster paints, crayons, colored paper, scissors and library paste. There were stories and games in a circle. They had a snack during class and a time to rest after the snack.

"I'll be looking forward to seeing everyone tomorrow." The teacher said.

"Tomorrow? You mean I have to come back again tomorrow?"

Sarah learned to love school even if she hadn't planned on returning the next day.

Chapter 4
September

It was a cold and rainy September morning in the mid nineteen fifties. The children were in the classroom coloring their September booklets. The cover of the booklet is a scene of the fall season as the leaves begin to fall from the trees. Children are running and playing as they return home from a day at school. They carry their books on their backs with book straps or in briefcases in their hands. It is near the end of the calendar year yet the beginning of another school year. Mrs. Gold had introduced these booklets as study aids for her third grade classroom. It was something new for the children to do when they had some quiet time. There were exercises inside to help with language development and also some other activities such as picture and number puzzles to be worked on at home.

There was no instruction as to how to color the covers of the booklets, each pupil was to use his or her own imagination to complete it. It was a complicated drawing for eight year olds to color.

Sarah remembered that booklet throughout her lifetime. When it was completed it was her most treasured work of art. She loved it even more than the aquarium painting that won her a prize in a regional art contest. It was more than a picture to be colored, it was a work to be completed in her own way at her own pace. No grade was given for this project, it was truly her own.

Where is that booklet today? Long gone; but the principles and the learning given to her by Mrs. Gold are carried along in everything she does.

Third grade. The beginning of real learning. The start of cursive writing instruction. The start of reading for comprehension, of learning multiplication tables, the laying down of skills that opened a treasure trove of possibilities. One who can read can learn anything. That's what Mrs. Gold told them. All knowledge was now available for anyone who could employ the code of letters, numbers and words.

Mrs. Gold worked after school hours to think of projects for her class to do. Sometimes her husband helped her to design projects as well. They designed a cardboard loom to be used for a weaving project. Each student wove a place mat that could be lifted off the cardboard when the weaving was finished. The students each were able to choose their own colors of yarn and plan their own designs.

Oh, the pleasure of being eight years old and having no expectation of how projects would turn out! The fun of filling in the pages of pristine notebooks at the start of the school year!

Sarah loved to fill her notebooks completely. I mean completely, including the margins which were filled with doodles and notes and the front and back inside covers which were filled with doodles and notes and the front and back outside covers whose marbleized designs were colored in with various colored inks and crayons to create new designs.

Mrs. Gold's classroom was dark and dreary even on sunny days. She had the class produce artwork to fill the tall windows at all times. Each season demanded new décor as they learned about the cycles of the seasons of the year. It was in this classroom that Sarah became a blackboard monitor. What a gift! She clapped the erasers in the yard after school and during recess. She washed the blackboards and learned how to write on the wet board to make the chalk colors more brilliant. She was happy to be one of the tallest children in the class so she might so this and write the headings for each day. Each morning she wrote the name of the day of the week, the date and a symbol indicating the weather for that day. She watched her work during the classroom time and cleaned it at the end of the day.

Mrs. Gold became a surrogate parent to Sarah. It was through contact with her and others like her that Sarah learned how adults other than Esther behaved. It was through such people that Sarah learned that the world need not be a hostile and frightening place, that learning new things and exploring new places could be positive and pleasant in nature, that it was good to expand one's horizons and set goals for the future.

So many baby boomers have fond memories of the smell of crayons in the classroom. This was Sarah's memory, the brightly colored cover of her September booklet, shiny, burnished and densely colored with Crayola crayons. Every millimeter of that page was colored. Sarah had filled it with colors and doodles that represented the idyllic world that might be possible if someone other than Esther were her mother.

Chapter 5
I Want My Ears Pierced

Sarah's closest childhood friends were two sisters whose mother was born in Puerto Rico. Every so often their family would take a trip to that tropical place. Naturally, the ideal time to do such a thing was in Midwinter at the time of the holidays.

The girls were aged one and four years when they returned from such a trip wearing earrings. They had had their ears pierced! If Ann and Jean could have theirs pierced, why couldn't Sarah have hers done, too? She begged her mother to take her and have it done or she would do it herself. She was four years old like her friend Ann. Esther told Sarah she could have it done but she would have to wait until she was older. During the waiting period, Sarah made careful mental noted of what type of earrings she wanted and kept a running list of children and adults she knew who had pierced ears. She even pierced the ears of her own dolls with safety pins thinking that, if all else failed, she could do the same for herself.

Esther and her older sisters had pierced ears. It was done when they were infants in Europe. That was the custom there. Pierced ears hadn't yet caught on in the United States. European immigrants were sensitive about anything that would single them out as being from somewhere else so they let the holes close over hoping no one would notice and identify them as greenhorns. The younger American girls born into Esther's family did not have pierced ears. They were Americans.

Sarah reluctantly agreed to wait. Her pediatrician would be the one to do the procedure. Each time she went to his office she'd ask if he would be doing the ear piercing. Each time she was told it wasn't time yet.

On a field trip to the Brooklyn Museum, Sarah learned about a culture where everyone had pierced ears. Men and women both had huge plugs in their ear lobes. When the plugs were removed, the earlobes hung down to their shoulders as the skin had stretched around the plugs. She asked how this was done and was told that each year or so, the person would get a larger plug to put in the earlobe until they had finally reached the maximum size without tearing through. Some were as big across as saucers. She wanted that.

In the school yard while the weather was still warm and the children were able to line up outside, Sarah observed the other little girls each day, checking for earrings. Every so often a new girl presented with newly pierced ears and pretty gold earrings in their lobes. Her friend Mara, who was two years older had hers done. The doctor had painted them with Mercurichrome. This really made them stand out. They were so red they looked as if they hurt. Mara assured Sarah that it wasn't painful at all, it only looked that way.

After many years of waiting, none of them patiently, Sarah's time finally arrived. She was nine years old. She went to the doctor's office on Columbus Day and had her ears pierced. Before the procedure he sent her and her mother off to a jewelry store to buy a pair of golden earrings so he might put them in after the piercing was done. The earrings they chose were gold wires with hearts. Excitedly, Sarah headed back to the doctor's office, earrings in her hand. Dr. Fiore explained that first he would pierce the ears with a needle and surgical thread and then place the earring in the hole made by the thread. He showed her the catgut thread. Knowing she was allergic to Mercurichrome he promised he would not use that on her ears.

She sat perfectly still in the chair while he prepared her earlobes with antiseptic but without anaesthetic. She sat perfectly still as he approached her earlobe with the needle and the suture. She heard the sound of the needle as it popped through her earlobe. It didn't hurt much at all. It was the sound that made her leap from her seat and run into the waiting room with the catgut suture dangling from her earlobe.

"I'm not going back in there!"

"You have to have the other ear done."

"No, I don't. I'll live this way with one ear pierced."

"It looks very strange."

" I don't care. I won't go back in there."

Sarah sobbed hysterically until Dr. Fiore came out to convince her to return. She couldn't explain to him that it was the sound of the needle that nauseated her. He thought it was the pain that bothered her.

"I can hear it."

"It's in your ear, I can't help that." He explained.

She finally agreed to go back into the office. She was sobbing so hard at this point that he was able to put the suture in the other ear without her even hearing it go in. He placed the earrings. It was done. She had pierced ears.

The next day at school she proudly wore her new earrings as she stood in line in the yard. It was getting cold, the weather was changing and fall was in the air. No matter. Sarah bared her earlobes for all to see. Another girl in a different class had also taken advantage of the holiday to have her ears pierced. Her ample lobes were bright red with Mercurichrome and chandelier shaped earrings dangled from them.

Every year at the times when the leaves begin to change color and the nip of fall weather is in the air, Sarah thinks of the lineup in the school yard and little girls with Mercurichrome colored earlobes.

Those really were good days. She was in fourth grade, in the yard with the upper grades. Her teacher, Mrs. Mann was still being nice to her. She hadn't started to shame her in front of the other children. She even had invited her to her apartment to meet Mr. Mann and to see her collection of Delft china from Holland which she brought back from her last trip to Europe. She had a pair of Delft earrings she often wore to school. They were for pierced ears. Mrs. Mann had been born in Europe, too but didn't feel any need to hide her pierced earlobes. The Delft earrings, with scenes of windmills on them were very heavy and had pulled her earlobes down , distorting the holes into long slits. They looked like they would pull through the skin at any moment. Sarah felt bad for her and her burden.

By the next year Sarah had tried to convince Esther to get larger and larger diameter earrings for her to wear to begin the stretching process. Esther thought that was a barbaric idea and soon squelched it. Friends of theirs, a sweet older couple gave Sarah a pair of sterling silver earrings as a gift. As soon as she put them on, she developed a reaction to them which eventually led to a painful infection. With the infection came the folk medicine treatments for them. Aunt

Fay who had let her piercings close up was a great critic. When Esther tried to drain Sarah's ears using hot packs and Sarah complained of the pain, Fay informed her that beauty always comes with a price. Sarah wasn't thinking of beauty, only about a way to wear earrings that were larger and larger each year until her earlobes would hang down to her shoulders without splitting.

Chapter 6
Dish Night

It's a Wednesday night and the line to get into the Beverly Theater extends down the block as far as the fruit and vegetable store. It's dish night and the local homemakers are waiting to get in to get the free dishes.

Sarah and her friends Ann and Jean are on line with Ann and Jean's mother, Hilda. Hilda had invited as many of her daughters' friends as she could to go to the movies so she could get more dishes. The girls didn't mind, she paid for their tickets and they got to see some good movies. There was a period of time when they went every week until the whole set was collected.

Dish towels were given out in boxes of laundry detergent. Hilda collected those, too.

The children only wanted to collect the toys which were found in boxes of cereal but Hilda caught on when the cereal boxes were empty after only one serving. She was in favor of a good offer but you had to use the product, too.

Ann and Jean were a curiosity to Sarah. Their mother was from Puerto Rico, a Christian, married to a man who was a Spanish Jew. Sarah was curious about Hilda's life and her religious beliefs although once she made the mistake of saying in front of her that Hilda was a Catholic and this produced a lot of hostility from Hilda. Sarah never stated that again although she didn't understand what the problem was. Wasn't every Christian a Catholic? She had no knowledge of the difference between Christian denominations as Jews were simply Jews whether orthodox, conservative or reform. Well…the reformed Jews weren't really Jews in the eyes of Sarah's parents; they might as well be Goyim.

Didn't they allow men in the synagogue without head covering? Didn't they eat non-kosher food and work on the Sabbath? What kind of Jew would do these things? Answer: a Goy.

At any rate, Ann and Jean's dad was a Sephardic Jew whose family spoke Spanish instead of Yiddish as Sarah's family did. His mother spoke only Spanish, no English at all although she looked like an old Jewish woman. Senora Luria was very quiet, severe in her dress and elderly looking beyond her years. She was the opposite of Hilda's mother who was a youthful looking Spanish woman, friendly and outgoing. Although her native tongue was Spanish, she spoke fluent English and loved to have Ann and Jean's friends over to her apartment to give them treats and toys . Anna Lopez was a wonderful grandma, even to children who were not her relatives.

Looking at Anna Lopez, one could not imagine the tragedy she had experienced in her life. Her first husband, Hilda's father died at a young age leaving her a young widow with two small children. She married a second time. This man was a medical doctor. He, too died at an early age leaving her widowed for a second time. Her third man was an American . They didn't marry. He was introduced as her "friend". They stayed together for years. She loved him and felt marriage to her carried the death penalty. He was like a grandpa to the girls although they always called him "Grandma's friend Jack".

Life at the Luria's apartment was always lively. Hilda was a master interior decorator. She constantly tried out new styles of furniture, wallpaper and floor coverings. Her husband was handy and helped her redo her kitchen several times. She read a lot of magazines about decorating and liked to have the latest trend in her own home. They were so different from Sarah's parents. That was why Sarah spent so much time with them.

Isaac Luria did not want his wife to work outside the home, just as Sarah's dad but Isaac let Hilda work at Macy's during the holiday season to earn a little money to help pay for Christmas presents and to get the store discount given to employees. Often, the girls would all go to Macy's to see Hilda at the pocketbook counter and to watch her sell things to customers. They were very proud of her. She became a celebrity in the neighborhood. "Don't forget to ask for Hilda when you go shopping at Macy's. She'll help you find some nice gifts."

Hilda was much younger than Sarah's mother, Esther. She was in her twenties when the girls were born. Sarah joined Girl Scouts and had Hilda as her leader, too. She was asked to call her "Mrs. Luria" rather than Hilda. It took a little getting used to although Ann and Jean were still allowed to call her "Mom."

The Lurias had a Christmas tree every year. That was an object of fascination to Sarah as was the whole idea of Santa Claus and presents and all of the other decorations at Christmastime. Sarah was allowed to visit and to look at the tree, even help to trim it. She never asked for one of her own. After all, she wasn't a Christian. In the neighborhood she lived in, it was the Christians who were in the minority.

Ann and Jean learned to benefit from their parents' mixed marriage. They had all the holidays off from school and got presents for both Chanukah and Christmas. Sarah strongly doubted they understood what any of the religious stuff was about as she knew she was confused as well.

One year Sarah's Aunt Rachel decided she wanted to have a Christmas tree. Why? Why weren't people happy with who they were? Everyone wanted to be something else.

Everyone wanted to be something else as this was America in the nineteen-fifties and anything was possible. World War II and the Korean Conflict were over. The McCarthy era was over. It was the time of the Cold War and although the president was a war hero he was determined to keep the peace and restore stability to the country. Economic growth and education were encouraged. How else could we beat the Russians in space travel? People who were able to move relocated from the city to the suburbs where houses were popping up like mushrooms after the rain. Many of Sarah's relatives took advantage of this exodus as they settled in such wildernesses as East Meadow and Montauk Long Island.

Sarah and her parents would never dream of moving from the city they loved. That's what Sarah believed. The reality was that they were so poor they couldn't move from their rent-controlled apartment.

When Sarah attended college, she discovered she and her parents belonged to the social stratum known as the "lower middle-class" (or was it the "upper lower-class?"). This astonished her as she never thought of herself as a poor person. She was not poor, she had everything anyone would want. Having more money brought more problems. Having money meant you had to worry about others stealing what you had. What was truly valuable was something that could never be taken away; her curiosity and hunger to learn new things.

Her parents had lived through the Great Depression and the War. They had learned to subsist on very little. Sarah learned these lessons well, yet Esther made fun of Hilda when she collected the free dishes from the movie theater and the free towels from the detergent boxes. Esther resented these things for she felt they were "handouts" to the poor people of the neighborhood given to them to entice them to do something they weren't planning to do, such as see a movie.

If Esther wanted to see a movie, she would see it and not go for the free dishes. She had her pride, you know. Just because you were poor you didn't have to act poor. "Pride goeth before the fall" she would say and she kept on falling.

Chapter 7
The Middle Years

Sarah loved school. She felt as if she was born to be a student. Every subject was fun and being with the other children was a great relief from the constant surveillance of her parents, especially Esther.

Esther made a valiant effort to keep Sarah at home as much as possible. When Sarah was the slightest bit ill, she was kept at home sometimes for weeks at a time. What Esther wanted was company at home and an audience for her interminable stories.

Esther completed her need for attention with the manipulation of food to demonstrate love. If Sarah loved her she would eat everything she prepared for her. If she didn't eat it all, the only conclusion was that she did not love her mother. She was asked, "How was that?" If she replied that it was good, that was not good enough. Superlatives were required in each case or she was never let off the hook.

Needless to say, Sarah was a fat child. Her greatest wish was for her mother's happiness even if that meant she would be teased by other children. She viewed herself as the source of happiness or unhappiness for her mother. Later in life, much, much later she learned nothing would ever make her mother happy.

Sarah developed a sense of humor as fat children are wont to do to cover up their sadness when teased by other children who saw only the fat girl and not a child, like themselves who wanted to have friends.

As long as Esther took Sarah to school, she made the decision whether or not Sarah went on any particular day. Sarah did not want to defy her mother and go to school against her wishes. The visit from the truant officer helped Sarah immensely. From then on, Sarah went to school when she wanted.

After school was a pleasant time, much like school. She would go out to play with her friends and wait for Daddy to come home from work. She could see him as he came down the block every evening at ten after five. She would say goodnight to her friends and head into the house with Daddy.

Sarah loved to act and sing. Her mother nicknamed her "Sarah Heartburn" for this tendency. It would have been a great feeling to get up in front of an audience to entertain them but a shy fat girl didn't like to do that except in front of those she knew wouldn't laugh at her size.

She envied those cute little children who looked adorable in whatever they wore. They were short and thin and had lots of pretty clothes. They were not as smart in school but they were popular. Sarah knew her strength was in working hard and learning as much as she could about everything. She sopped up the material like a sponge and asked for more.

At home, schoolwork was not held in high esteem. Esther had not been a good student. Her excuse was that she was born left-handed and was switched to the right hand in school. That explained her distinctive handwriting. She was more than happy to leave school after the eighth grade as school had nothing more to offer her. Sarah couldn't imagine school having nothing to offer. She wanted to go to school forever.

In her friends' homes, Sarah experienced parenting in a style to which she would have liked to become accustomed. Certain parents didn't mind if their children didn't clean their plates or if they ate in front of the TV. They didn't expect their children to clean the bathroom floor or do their laundry in the kitchen sink. There were also families who had money to pay for music lessons and other extras for the children.

There was a piano in Sarah's apartment. Her Daddy played it. She wanted piano lessons but they could not afford to pay for them. Sometimes she picked up some music and tried to learn to read it. Mostly, she played by ear, reproducing tunes she had heard on the radio and only when Daddy wasn't around as she didn't want his criticism. He was the pianist, not Sarah. When she became old enough to get the courage to ask him for lessons, he reluctantly agreed to teach her. Neither of them wanted him to help her with the piano in the way he had helped her with math! Math had changed since he had learned it and it had become a source of confusion and frustration for both of them. There were too many tears associated with math help.

Piano was different. There were no tears. When he taught, she understood and learned to enjoy her lessons. He told her he had started lessons himself at an advanced age, sixteen. She was ten and even that seemed old as her friends had been studying for years and were far advanced in their playing.

Things had improved in their living situation, too as when she was seven they had moved into a new apartment.

The apartment was in the same building, on the ground floor. The new apartment had three separate rooms so Esther had a real kitchen for the first time. Mother and Dad kept the convertible sofa and slept in the living room. Sarah had the bedroom for herself. The room divider that had separated the kitchen area from the living room in the studio apartment on the third floor was placed in Sarah's room. She turned it around so that the shelves faced outward into the room. One shelf became her desk. She chose fabric to make curtains to cover the other shelves when they were not in use. The fabric was white, printed with red and blue lipstick tubes and powder puffs. Daddy said it was a very "girly" type of print. She was proud. She was growing up.

They bought a new television, a sixteen inch set. The old twelve inch set was given to Sarah to keep in her room. She now had a desk and a television. Her life became complete when she found a stray kitten outside her window. After asking around to see who he belonged to and learning no one had claimed him, she was allowed to keep him. He was her dearest pet, friend and confidante. It was through the cat that Mrs. Ryan, her second grade teacher became Sarah's friend as well. She came to Sarah's home bringing Cat Fancy magazines and visiting with her. She was the first adult professional Sarah had as a friend and remained such throughout the time Sarah attended elementary school.

Those years of growing and learning were good year in spite of her mother's difficult personality. Most of the time, her parents argued with each other and it rarely had anything to do with her so she could retreat to her room and read, watch TV or do a craft project.

She knew she would grow up one day but that day was far off in the future. Her doctor said she was normal in spite of her scoliosis and her overweight. He said she would lose her "baby fat" as she grew older. He didn't know about her mother's use of food as a weapon.

In spite of her mother's behavior about food, Sarah was able to control some of what she ate on her own. School lunches which her mother packed did not have to be eaten, they could be thrown out! Lunch time might be a time for exercise, for socialization rather than simply a time to eat.

She recalled a particularly humiliating experience in fourth grade. Her teacher did not like her and certain other children in the class. She made fun of the way Sarah's mother dressed her. In one painful moment she made Sarah stand up in front of the class and showed the class how she was wearing long cotton stockings held up with garters on a garter belt to keep her legs warm in the winter. The stockings were equally hated by Sarah but there was nothing she could do about it. Her mother wanted her to wear them. Her mother also made her wear both a scarf and a hat, wrapping the scarf around her mouth to keep the wind out. The teacher also described to the class how Sarah looked wearing that as she walked to school.

In this case, her mother went to school and asked for Sarah to be removed from that classroom. The Principal made Sarah admit that her mother was a "nervous person" and didn't always describe things as they were. He said she tended to "dramatize" events and to give them more importance than they deserved. Sarah agreed with him but said that in this case, her mother was not exaggerating. She wanted to be moved from that classroom as soon as she could. The Principal explained that a new class would not be the same kind of class as the one she was in. She expressed to hope that he was right. He said he meant that the students were not as bright as the ones in the class she was leaving. She told him that was fine, she would make the adjustment.

The new class was wonderful in comparison, a real breath of fresh air. The teacher was a motherly woman who understood the trauma Sarah had suffered. Sarah made many new friends in that classroom. A great burden was lifted from her even though it wasn't hers to bear. She had heard of teachers being strict and difficult in their academic expectation but she never expected to be exposed to a teacher who would ridicule a child publicly in front of the class because of social differences over which the child had no control.

Chapter 8
The Very Last Day

Her parents fought constantly. She wondered why they stayed together. It was Esther's campaign to keep Adam alive against all odds for she hated his sister and the rest of his family for even doubting she could accomplish this.

"Adam is sick", they cried, "he can't be expected to live for very much longer." they cried and cried.

Esther did whatever she could to insure his health, although tenuous, would hold out. She religiously kept his salt-free diet. She made sure he took is blood pressure medication and lived with the depression it caused him. She would not do anything to jeopardize his health except she argued with him constantly!

The arguments were about silly things, like whose family was better or smarter or more successful. There was little money available so luxuries were out of the question most of the time. Often the arguments were about a purchase that was thought to be extravagant such as a high-priced roast when company was coming or a new pair of kitchen curtains for the same event.

Esther had to prove she was a good housekeeper even on the tightest budget. Working outside the home was out of the question. Adam forbade it. A man whose wife works is a poor provider. His wife would never work no matter how badly they needed the money.

Sarah was used to disappointment. She would ask her parents if they somewhere and plans would be made only to be broken as one or the other of them was not feeling well. Although there was nothing physically wrong with Esther, she developed high blood pressure when Adam made her pressure "go up" during their arguments.

Esther had also developed a skin condition when Sarah was born. She had washed Sarah's diapers in Tide detergent and reacted to the detergent with a case of eczema which lasted seven years. She wore cotton gloves at night to keep medicated cream on her hands so healing might occur while she slept. During the day she wore rubber gloves over the cotton gloves as she slaved at housework, growing flushed as her blood pressure rose with her increasing anger at having to do it at all. It goes without saying although she had used Tide only once, the reaction went on a lot longer.

Adam offered to hire a person to help with the housework if it would help heal Esther's hands. Each time a woman came to clean, Esther worked twice as hard; once before the cleaning woman came so she would not think Esther kept a messy house, the second time as Esther cleaned right along with her to show her how to do it properly.

Esther was as insecure about her domestic skills as her mother and sisters were proficient in theirs.

Grandma Rivka, Esther's mother sewed all the clothes for the family, knitted their sweaters, hats and socks, churned her own butter, made her own pickles, preserves and canned goods, kept her house spotless and daily served at least twelve people at her table at every meal. This was when she lived in

America. Who knew what she did in Europe? Perhaps she milked her own cow. Who dared to ask?

Her other daughters were equally accomplished except for Esther who never learned how to do such domestic chores and for Lydia, the ultra-spoiled last child who was born when Rivka was forty -two years old.

Esther's sister Fay was eighteen when she married her childhood sweetheart. Her first child was born a year later, the same time as her mother's last child so Sarah had an aunt and cousin who were both grown women when she was born.

"It's time to stop having babies," declared Rivka when Lydia was born. She threw her husband out of the bedroom. Lydia was the last child at home and very disobedient. It was Lydia's baby who was given up for adoption the year bfore Sarah was born.

Every family get-together was a contest to determine who was the best hostess and who had the most beautiful home and served the most delicious meal. Esther always came up short.

After her husband, the Rabbi died, grandma Rivka stayed with Lydia until she couldn't stand it any longer. A second child was born after the son who was given up for adoption. Lydia kept this little boy. Rivka helped her raise him until Lydia found a husband. The one she found was like her, an alcoholic who spent his days drinking and crying. When Rivka had had enough she moved in with the other daughters, one at a time for various periods of time.

Esther wondered why Rivka did not want to live with her. The other sisters had much larger homes with more resources to care for their aging mother. Esther had nothing but an insecurity that would not rest. She had to prove she could care for her mother as well as her sisters could.

One fateful day Rivka moved in with Esther, Adam and Sarah and shared Sarah's beautiful sleigh bed. Sarah was eleven years old. She had always wanted someone to share her room but thought it might be a younger sibling. She was not prepared to share it with an eighty-three year old woman.

When Rivka moved in, she became a source of irritation to Adam. Possibly he was upset about the way Esther had treated his mother compared to the way she treated her own.

The fighting increased in frequency and volume; but now Sarah had no haven for escape. Her room was occupied. She became fast friends with her Grandma who recognized her situation and need for refuge. They began to go on outings together.

Although Grandma was very deaf, her eyes were bright and sharp. Sarah could not see a far or as clearly as Rivka. They took long walks to get away from the house and spent many happy hours window shopping on Flatbush Avenue. Often, they stopped at Garfield's cafeteria for lunch. Sarah's cousins and friends made fun of her for being so close to such an old-fashioned woman. In spite of that, the two of them understood their need to stand together while all about their lives was chaos.

One glorious day Adam bought a car, It was a used car, a 1958 Oldsmobile. The car was silver with a red roof and red upholstery. He called it "The Redhead" after Lucille Ball whose show "I Love Lucy" was the hit of the time. The car was his pride and joy and he loved to park it on the street near their windows so he might see it at all times. He was so pleased he was able to learn to drive at his advanced age of fifty and he was feeling even better physically. The doctor had placed him on a new medication for his blood pressure, called "Hydro-diuril," and his pressure was in much better control. This medication did not cause depression. It was truly a miracle drug!

A car in the city is looked at, not used daily. It must be moved for alternate-side –of-the-street parking but that is most of its activity. It was to be used for trips out of the city. When Adam got the car in May, he planned short trips with the family. As he became a more experienced driver, his scope widened to include trips upstate to visit friends who had moved away from the city life.

The Redhead was a wonderful thing. Daddy was so proud of it. He had a bottle of touch-up paint in silver and one in red to repair any tiny scratch that might mar the perfection of his new love. He polished it constantly and kept it in pristine condition.

They took a trip to Newburgh, New York to see the sights in the country and to stay overnight in a motel. It was the first time they had done such a thing and Sarah was thrilled beyond belief to see a place other than Brooklyn and to wake up to the sights and smells of a Catskill mountain morning.

While on the trip, Adam became ill. He developed some pain he described as "indigestion". Reluctantly, he went to a local doctor's office for treatment as he was to drive home that day and all were concerned for his health. The doctor heard the heart murmur when he examined him. A medication was prescribed which Adam picked up at a pharmacy and put in his pocket in case he might need it. He continued to complain of chest pain. Esther asked if he had taken the medication. Adam replied that he hadn't. It remained unopened in his pocket. That was the beginning of the end.

When they got home, Esther confided in Sarah. She said the doctor had told her Adam was very sick and could die at any time. He hoped this would happen while he was asleep so Esther would be spared seeing him suffer as there was nothing medical science could do to remedy his condition.

Sarah couldn't believe what she had heard. Hadn't Daddy lived such a long time with his heart condition, far beyond what anyone had expected? He was feeling so much better now, his blood pressure and depression no longer a problem. That doctor frightened them with what he said. Daddy must not know about it!

A week later, he had an attack of the "flu". His own doctor treated him and when it was over, pronounced him well enough to go back to work. All he wanted to know was if he would be able to drive his car. The doctor gave him permission to do so.

On that last day, they went to Staten Island for a picnic. In those days, the late nineteen-fifties, before the Verrazano Bridge was built, the best was to get to Staten Island from Brooklyn was by a ferry which ran from Battery Park in Manhattan. They had to cross into Manhattan via the Brooklyn Bridge, then board the ferry to Staten Island.

Esther had packed a picnic lunch in a large metal cooler which sat on the floor of the car in the back, right in front of Sarah. It had been their usual custom to sit, all three of them in the front seat; but Sarah had to sit in the back that day because of her swollen left arm.

When they had returned from their Catskill trip, Sarah was not feeling well herself. She thought she might have hay fever. After much pleading, she was taken to the doctor for allergy testing. Reluctantly, the doctor gave her a test on her left arm. As he injected to allergen, her arm began to swell. She was instructed to sit in the doctor's waiting room for fifteen minutes to see how the test progressed. By then the swelling had extended from just below her shoulder across the elbow joint and down to the wrist. The doctor remarked that he had never seen such a dramatic reaction in such a short time. She was given antihistamines and sent home. The swelling made it uncomfortable for her to sit in the front seat of the car between her parents so she sat in the back with a pillow under her arm. Even though the swelling was much better by Labor Day, she was advised by her parents she was better off to stay in the back with the cooler.

The last day was the best day! Her parents didn't argue at all. Not even one tiny disagreement. The lunch they had brought was perfect. Sarah was so happy. The weather, the place, the emotional climate all had conspired to make this a perfect way to end the summer. She had put the doctor's prediction out of her conscious mind as Daddy looked and felt better than he had in several weeks.

They cleared away the lunch things and brought them back to the car for the return trip to Brooklyn via the ferry to Manhattan. The ferry ride was fun. They stood next to the car and took pictures with Sarah's Brownie Hawkeye camera. Sarah and her father liked to stand as close as possible to the ferry ropes so they might watch the waves and be sprayed by the salty spray of the river as its water mingled with that of the ocean.

They drove off the ferry at Battery Park. They stopped for a while to feed the pigeons and to check for directions for the next part of the trip back home. They go on the road, looking for the sign for the Brooklyn Bridge. How many times did they pass the same place and miss that sign? Each time they came near it, it seemed to vanish. How frustrating! It was such a simple thing. One saw the bridge but could not find the approach to it.

After many attempts, Daddy found the turnoff to the bridge. He was in the left lane of traffic on the bridge when Sarah heard a strange scraping noise. It was their car scraping along the metal barrier on the side of the bridge. She heard it again. Daddy slumped over as he was driving and she saw her mother using her newly learned driving skills to try to steer the car away from the side of the bridge. There wasn't much traffic that afternoon. The person in the car behind them had seen the driver ahead slump down so he knew the car was in trouble. Sarah looked at the car in front of them and knew they were about to crash into it. It was a white car, just like the one she had seen in a dream a few days before. "We're going to crash" she heard herself say as she had said in the dream; but this time it was really happening.

The driver in the white car was alone and was not hurt. Thank God!

Sarah looked over the back of the front seat when the car stopped. The impact of the crash had pushed the front seat back toward her where she held on to the top of the seat to brace herself at the time of the collision. Her father wasn't moving. He was very pale and had a tiny cut under his chin that wasn't bleeding. Her mother was unconscious, murmuring something. She was alive. The police came and took her father away, placing a sheet over his face. They lay her mother on the side of the road on a coarse woolen blanket. It was hot on that pavement. It was two-thirty in the afternoon.

The driver of the white car was upset. The police spoke with him and gave him some information. They towed both cars away.

Sarah stood by the side of the road with her mother who was now regaining consciousness. She carried the cooler as well as her purse and her mother's purse. She clung to these things as they were all she had to connect her to the life she had until moments ago. She was wearing her favorite shoes, a pair of cream colored moccasins with gray tassels and gray rubber soles. The purse she carried was a gift for her twelfth birthday that July, just two months before. The gift was from Lula Lieber, her friend Janie's mother. In that purse was anything anyone needed to know about her. She'd have to show her address and phone number to the people at the hospital. They took her and her father to Cumberland Hospital and her mother to Kings County.

She rode in the ambulance with her father's body, the cooler and her purse. She had given up her mother's purse to the driver of the other ambulance. They took her to a place in the hospital that was a waiting room. Waiting for what? Some attendants came in carrying her father's clothing in a little pile and placed it on a desk.

"I undressed that man that was brought in, Here are his things."

The attendant was told those things needed to stay with the body.

"Why didn't they tell me first, he's heavy."

They looked at Sarah. She had gotten up to wash a place on her arm that was bleeding. She was hardly injured at all. All she wanted to do was go home. She knew she could get there if they would let her. They wouldn't. She had to be examined before they would let her go.

"I'll examine her", said one of the attendants, grinning and making an obscene gesture.

Someone did examine her and dressed the cut on her arm. Her uncle came for her. She wanted to go to her house, not his. He insisted she go with him. He had brought fortifications, his brother-in-law. They were both drunk, as usual, except today there was a reason to be drinking this early in the day. They took Sarah and the cooler into her uncle's car and headed for his house where she would spend the night.

How could she sleep that night? Where was her mother? Was she still alive? What about her father? Was he really dead or were they able to perform a miracle at the hospital. What would happen to her?

If they hadn't missed the turn for the bridge they might have been at home now, all of them. Daddy would die peacefully in his bed as the doctor had said.

If she could go home now, maybe she would find this was all a bad dream. Maybe she would awaken in her own bed and discover that none of this had ever happened.

No, she knew it wasn't a dream.

Chapter 9
Have No Fear

"Death doesn't frighten me anymore" thought Adam as he read his Bible. After the episode with the doctor in Newburgh, he knew it wasn't going to be long before death would come for him.

He had devised a plan which he told Esther. He wouldn't die alone; he would take his family with him as he couldn't bear to be parted from those he loved. Esther was furious. "How could he think of such a selfish thing?" she said. He knew it wouldn't be unkind to remove them from this world of troubles along with himself whose time was rapidly running out. He believed in God. He knew God would be kind to him and take him quickly. After all, he had suffered a long time in his lifetime. How much more would he suffer in death? Death was the end: The end of suffering, the end of pain.

Sarah saw his doodles by the telephone. Daddy always doodled when he spoke on the phone. Mostly they were cubes and boxes, geometric designs that he filled in and shaded to give them dimension. Lately they had taken on the distinct shapes of coffins and tombstones.

She was frightened. Had Esther told him what the doctor had said about dying in his sleep? She hoped not. She did everything she could to keep it from him herself; but who knew? Maybe he had asked the doctor himself.

That morning Adam sat on the sofa bed watching TV. He was unshaven, wearing his favorite striped pajamas. Sarah sat next to him. They didn't speak. They looked at each other in silence. Later that morning he would get up and shave to get ready for their picnic on Staten Island. It was Labor Day, September 7, 1959.

The day was the best he had had in a long time. He felt well. The chest pain wasn't too bad, not enough to keep him from enjoying a family picnic. Esther was in a good mood, too. She had been refraining from arguments ever since his illness in Newburgh. He thought it had something to do with his starting to read the Bible after many years. He was reading "Proverbs" and telling her how a good wife was a treasure worth more than jewels. He had recovered from the "flu" over the past week and hadn't been to work that week. Tomorrow he would return to his job at the shipping company. Today was a holiday.

Things were certainly improving in his life. He now had enough money to buy some little luxuries that others in his family had enjoyed for years. Didn't Morris and Herman have cars? Morris, his oldest brother was the owner of a successful hardware store in New Jersey. At the first opportunity he and his wife had moved to the Garden State. Their daughter attended private college and became a schoolteacher like her mother. They had everything and never hesitated to verify that fact.

Herman had a good job, too. His hobby was photography. He was good enough to make it his career ; but since he too had a family to support, he didn't want to take the risk of becoming self-employed. They lived in a neat little brick house near Brooklyn College. Just as he had resisted starting his own business, he resisted buying the house they lived in. They continued to rent. The Depression had made him vary of taking monetary risks. He had a car as well. His oldest son was now old enough to drive it.

Adam's neighbor Isaac Luria had bought a new car in 1957. It was one of those Chevy's with tail fins. Adam loved that car and talked with Isaac about learning to drive so he might have one too. Isaac helped him as he helped everyone. It was his nature to be kind. He offered to take Adam for a ride in the new car with Sarah and his daughters, Ann and Jean. Adam was hooked. He wanted a car.

Now, he had his own car. She was a beauty, a 1958 Oldsmobile with very little mileage. What great fortune! He had even started giving private piano lessons to friends as a side business. Mostly, he liked to teach adults or older teenagers who were beginners. He was teaching Sarah who had wanted to learn for years. "I seem to be developing more patience as I get older. She helps me understand what I need to do to teach others. If I can be patient with her, I can be a better teacher for everyone."

The picnic that day was planned but not too far in advance. Esther had time to prepare lunch which she put in the new cooler. The cooler was roomy. It had a compartment on top where you put special packets of ice. The cooler was insulated like a thermos bottle to keep things cold or warm. It was made of metal and heavy to carry. It was big enough to place things on while eating, a table of sorts. It was the state of the art.

Adam and Sarah loved boat rides. Hadn't they done the Circle Line cruise around Manhattan island? Why not take the Staten Island Ferry and have a picnic in a park on

Staten Island? That would make everyone happy as Esther adored picnics. She reminded him often of how she used to live in the country and hated the seashore and the ocean. Adam loved the ocean and hated the country. He'd rather go to the beach any day than sit in a park. He decided this day to please Esther.

The ferry ride both ways was as pleasant as ever. It was as if nature had conspired to make this a perfect day. They stopped at Battery Park to feed the pigeons. Adam laughed to himself. He thought it must be genetic how all his family members liked to feed pigeons. He thought of his sister, Leah, her fingertips permanently stained red from the dyed pistachio nuts she fed to the pigeons from the vending machines in the subway station while waiting for her train to Brighton Beach. Sarah enjoyed it, too. Many happy days were spent feeding those little freeloaders wherever they went. He felt sorry for them, living in the city, roosting on buildings instead of trees which were their natural homes. His family had always lived in cities. Esther's was from the countryside in Russia. He supposed that was why she loved the pastoral setting so much. His family was from Odessa on the Black Sea. They were merchants. They moved to Brighton Beach when they emigrated and stayed there as it was so much like Odessa.

After the pigeon feeding, it was time to head home. He hadn't had much discomfort at all that day. Perhaps he was wrong in thinking his life was ending. He got into the car and started toward the entrance for the bridge.

Where was it? He knew it had to be nearby. Where was the sign?

"Look, Daddy, there's the sign for the Brooklyn Bridge" Sarah called from the back seat of the car. He saw it as he passed it, turning away from the bridge.

"I'm getting to be like Morris", he thought. "He's the only man who lives in Jersey who can get lost in the Holland Tunnel every time! How many years would he have to live there before he would get it right?" Now, he understood how confusing those signs could be to drivers. There was no time to stop and look at them as when you were walking.

Finally, finally he found the sign for the approach to the bridge and he got into the correct traffic lane.

Then everything disappeared. Where was his car, his family, the bridge? Where was the pain in his chest? Where was his body?

He saw it all, the accident on the bridge, the ambulance people taking his body into their vehicle. He saw them put a sheet over his face.

"That's it? That's all that happens?" He was confused as he watched his body riding away in the ambulance with Sarah sitting at his side. He hoped the whole family would be together; but he was alone. He was not really alone. A crowd of relatives was waiting for him on the Manhattan side of the bridge. He had to turn back, to go with them. There was no choice. They assured him his wife and daughter would be taken care of, that they were no longer his responsibility. He had other things to do now. "How selfish I've been", he thought "to want to take them with me." He understood it was not his decision to make no matter how much he wanted to be with them.

"I have to get a message to them. I have to let them know I am all right, that I have no pain and I am not tired any longer; but I have no body! How can I tell them?"

His mother and father stood beside him while he watched the scenes surrounding his death. "We have to take you with us now, there are things to do and new things to learn."

For many years after that day, Sarah searched for him in her dreams. She waited for a sign, a sign he wanted to give her that he was all right and no longer in pain. Sometimes he was able to come through to let her know he was thinking of her; but then he would disappear. Sometimes she thought she heard his footsteps in the hall or saw him in a crowd only to remember he was really gone.

After a while she couldn't keep the memory of his face in her mind and she felt as though she had betrayed him. How could she forget what he looked like? How could she forget the sound of his voice?

She moved away from that apartment years later. She married, started a family and a career. Sometimes he seemed to be very close, as on her wedding day or the day her first son was born, she named him after Adam. He looked like him in the baby picture Sarah kept of her father taken in 1909. No surprise, they all look alike in our family!

Where was he? When people die do they simply disappear? Do we cease to exist at the moment of physical death? The Bible says we will be resurrected at the last day when Messiah comes. Where do we stay until that day? The Psalmist has us sleeping underground in darkness. Is that what we do? What about the body? Why do we take such pains to insure nothing is removed from the body so we may be raised whole on the last day? What about those people who were cremated in the ovens in the Holocaust? What about those people not buried in graves who lost their lives in war?

Questions! She thought of her Grandpa, the one who had been a Rabbi. Surely he would have been able to answer her questions except he died when she was a baby. Where was he now?

Was her father looking for her as she was looking for him?

He was on his way toward the sun, or so he thought it was as he saw the brightest light one could imagine. Out of the light emerged the figure of one who looked like a man. He was so magnificent, everyone must bow before this glorious being.

Adam bowed his head in adoration before this holy being of light. As he bowed he heard the words, "I baptize you in the name of the Father and of the Son and of the Holy Spirit as it was in the beginning is now and will be forever, world without end, amen."

A flood of water washed over him and with it washed away all the cares and sins of his life on earth.

He was confused. Who was this being? He realized it was The Messiah himself who had saved him and given him eternal life.

"The Lord is my light and my salvation," he thought, "of whom then shall I be afraid?"

Chapter 10
The Black Armband

The front yards of the people who lived along Ocean Parkway were the miles of benches, the bicycle paths, the bridle paths which formed islands in the sea of traffic of the parkway, a six-lane highway with service lanes on either side of the road. Trees were planted on the islands of concrete to provide shade to the seemingly limitless expanse of pavement.

Sarah's first memory of this vista was of sitting in her baby carriage looking at her mother while her mother sat on a bench facing her, conversing with neighbors who also had young children in carriages.

Milestones of development and growth were marked by the activities done in this urban playground. First, the carriage, then the stroller; then out to the patches of earth around the trees to dig with shovels and make mudpies. The tentative first steps on roller skates, Sarah holding on the railing between the benches and the bicycle path as Daddy watched with pride and trepidation. The endless games of "hit the penny" played with the city concrete blocks as boundaries. The drawings made with sidewalk chalk at

Hallowe'en time. The meetings of the older kids at dusk as they watched the traffic, named the cars and the year of their manufacture. The snowmen built when there was some snow on the ground. The bicycle rides on the bicycle path that extended from Prospect Park to Coney Island.

All these marked the days of a child who lived on Ocean Parkway; but nothing could compare with the times twice yearly when the Parkway became an undulating sea of humans dressed for the most important days of the Jewish liturgical calendar, the High Holy Days.

Every Jewish person living on or near the Parkway was out on those days dressed in his or her finest fall outfit, an outfit bought traditionally for these celebrations. There was no work, no school, no business activity. The people walked up and down the streets greeting each other, wishing each other a Happy New Year. Transportation was by foot. No driving or riding was permitted. The masses headed toward the synagogues for prayers at sundown and in the mornings.

Sarah had read her Golden Bible from the time she was able to read words. Before that, she had delighted in the illustrations and asked her parents to explain what they were about. The Bible was her first and most loved book.

When she asked what all the people were doing in the streets on the Holy Days, she was told they were on their way to shul to pray. Her parents didn't go. They didn't have seats for the services. She asked if she might go to see what it was like in the shul. She wanted to hear more about God and the Bible.

On ordinary days of the year, Sarah and her friends liked to play on the steps of the Jewish Center. These Holy Days they were not allowed to play there as people crowded to get in.

The people with tickets filled the sanctuary seats. Others were standing in the back. Sarah peeked in as well as she could between the bodies of the standees. A man was singing a prayer in God's language, Hebrew. Sarah didn't understand the prayer but still loved the sound of the words and music.

The Rabbi started to pray in Hebrew and Sarah wished she knew what it meant.

She went home to her parents and asked how she might learn the Hebrew prayers. She was told one had to go to Hebrew school to do so.

"So, when do I start?"

"Start what?"

"Hebrew school?"

"Girls don't go to Hebrew school."

Sarah went to her room and cried, "What am I doing in this female body?"

Crying didn't change anything. She contented herself by reading the Bible in English.

Although she knew her grandfather had been a rabbi, she wondered why her parents didn't attend synagogue. They kept the rules of the faith including the laws of kashruth and the Sabbath; but they didn't belong to any temple, not even the one on the corner of their street. She thought it might have something to do with them being too poor to afford tickets for the services. The High Holy Day seats were expensive. If you were standing, people would know you couldn't pay and this would be a source of shame. In her neighborhood, there were more people standing than sitting.

Their little apartment was filled with people when her Daddy died. There were relatives she hadn't seen before or since, talking about him and his life. Where were they during his life? They were dressed like they would be for the High Holy Days although those were two weeks away.

The immediate family wore black armbands on the left arm, closer to the heart. The closest relatives had rips in the fabric to indicate their hearts were broken. She didn't need to wear the armband although she did comply. Her heart was completely broken in two and was plainly visible to anyone who saw her.

They sat on low wooden benches and mourned for seven days. The mirrors in their home were covered so there would be no vanity in the household.

She went outside to sit on her favorite bench on the Parkway.

School would be starting the week after the mourning period was over. He had died on Labor Day. This year Sarah was to start Junior High in a new school building. Few of her friends knew of her loss, most were away on vacation. Her mother offered her a new outfit to wear for the first day of school. It was the outfit she had bought for five dollars at a discount store so she would have something new to wear for the holidays.

Sarah looked up at the clouds to see if she could see her father. Was he in heaven yet? The funeral was over. He was buried in the ground. His grave would remain unmarked for another year as was the tradition. The clouds above were pink and gray. As she had done when she was smaller, she tried to make out figures in the shapes of the clouds. There was her cat, Fluffy. There was a rabbit or an elephant. There was an angel. Was it her father? She smiled. Maybe it was him. She cried. He was gone. Gone in an instant. Gone in a flash. One moment he was alive and then he wasn't.

Her mother had been hurt in the accident that followed when her father died while driving the car. She was at home recovering from her injuries. Sarah was caring for her. It was a lot for a twelve-year-old to do, but she was confident she could manage. Her mother was so frail, it always seemed she would be the one to die first. How ironic she would remain. Sarah told her mother they would get by and they did.

School started the Monday after the death. Sarah wore her mother's holiday outfit. It was a dark brown skirt with a brown and black striped top. Dark, serious, suitable for a girl in mourning.

There were no longer any relatives at the house to help out. They were alone. Sarah worried about her mother at home alone, still bruised badly from the accident. The children in the school cafeteria looked at her and whispered to each other. They thought she couldn't hear them when they said, "That's her. She's the one whose father died."

No one wanted to sit near her. They were afraid she might cry or they might have to say something to her and didn't know what the proper thing to say might be.

At home, Sarah and her mother ate the remaining food given to them by the relatives and friends after the funeral. Grandma Rivka sat in the living room watching TV, the volume turned up as high as it would go so she might hear.

"The shiva is over", she said "time to get back to normal."

Normal.

What was normal? Sarah felt as if a piece of her had been removed in a surgical procedure, a procedure so swift and clean no visible scar proved it had happened at all except the part that was missing left an invisible void that could neither be filled nor explained.

People tired of hearing about him. They didn't want to hear how his photograph developed a special light that surrounded him, singling him out from those in the photograph still among the living.

People tired of hearing how she or her mother dreamed about him; that in the dream he didn't know he had died and came back to his daily routine until someone mentioned they thought he had died and he would disappear.

How could he have left at this time, just when he was beginning to be happy? He owned a car! His blood pressure and depression were improved! He had even gone to the new hamburger stand and ate a burger and fries with salt because he was tired of the salt-free diet. Did he die because he ate a burger and fries with salt?

The autopsy report said he died of a cardiac tamponade from a ruptured aortic aneurysm and valve. It was the result of the infection he had suffered when he was a young child when he had Diphtheria. His death could not have been prevented at that time. There was no way to repair the damage to his heart in those days.

Two weeks after Labor Day the High Holy Days began.

The people lined the streets greeting each other and wishing each other the best for the New Year and another year's inscription in the Book of Life.

The shul was packed with worshippers. Just as the Christian churches have their Pointsettias and Easter Liles, people who come to services only at Christmas and Easter, the Jewish houses of worship have their Asters and Chrysanthemums who appear in the sacristy twice a year for required viewing at Rosh Hashanah and Yom Kippur, then fade into oblivion the rest of the liturgical year.

Sarah went out to her favorite bench again, wearing her mother's five dollar outfit. She looked at the sky to see if she could see him yet. Banks of fluffy clouds filled the bluest sky. There were dragons and monkeys, angels and trumpets and dogs and horses that smiled at her.

She was no longer wearing the black armband. The shiva was over. It was time to get back to normal.

How long would it take to do that?

How long is the period of mourning?

One year?

Four years?

Forty years?

Maybe forty times four…

Chapter 11
Jairus' Daughter

Almost one year had passed since Sarah's Daddy had died.

Esther thought it would be a good idea for them to take a cottage in the Catskills with Grandma Rivka for the summer.

They packed their things preparing to stay for the entire summer.

The cottage was charming, quite cozy and fully furnished. It was made of fieldstone and had a stone path leading to the front door. There were two bedrooms and a large room which functioned as a kitchen, sitting room and extra bedroom.

The bungalow colony of which the cottage was a part was a former estate. The owners lived year 'round in the big stone house and rented the smaller cottages to people from the city. The land bordered a lake and the colony had its own pier and dock.

The owners chose the tenants carefully, mindful of who would get along with whom for the summer months. It was an eclectic mix. A retired rabbi and his wife who knitted socks dried their laundry on the grass. A large multigenerational Italian family brought a grandmother who also spoke little English. A single woman from the city brought her grown daughter and her teenage boys.

Like any group of vacationing people, there were those who returned each year and those who were newcomers. The owners had friends in the town who came by to visit with them and socialize with the summer people as well.

It was unlike anything Sarah had previously experienced. To think that people lived anywhere other than the city was a new concept. There were no buses, subways and absolutely nothing to do at all but swim at the lake and visit with other people. The walk into town was about a mile down a country road. The town had a movie theater, a drugstore and a five and ten-cent variety store. There may have been other stores; but for Sarah those were the only interesting ones.

Sarah's Grandma Rivka and Grandma Volpi hit it off immediately. Neither of them spoke much English although between them was perfect understanding. Both were the oldest surviving members of immigrant families. They sat together remembering coming to America, of learning new ways and trying to raise families in a new culture. This respite from the city was a moment in time when they recalled their pastoral past lives before the world became crazy, before the World Wars and the Depression.

They sat happily watching the grandchildren play and shook their own heads at the ways of their adult children.

At night, Grandma talked in her sleep. She slept in the bedroom right next to Sarah's. Before Grandma went to sleep, she talked to herself. She was very deaf so she spoke loudly to someone who wasn't there. This was different from when she lived in Sarah's house and slept in her bed. Sarah thought it would be a relief not to have an octogenarian sharing her bed for the summer but the dialogue with the invisible person was "kind of creepy" to the thirteen-year-old. She tried to screen it out by listening to her portable radio. It was the radio Daddy gave her on her last birthday, the one before he died. The radio had been advertised extensively on TV. A man stood on a ladder and dropped the radio from it. "A radio with a portable 'impact' case." Her radio had fallen many times at home. She opened it after each such fall. It was just as the man on TV showed us. Nothing was broken inside.

"If only my life was like that radio." she thought, "If only our car had a portable 'impact' case. It would not have shattered in the accident the day Daddy died."

She hoped one day she would forget the accident. It was early, not even a full year had passed. The vision repeated of the car out of control, of her father, dead at the wheel, her mother, a non-driver trying to steer the car away from the side of the road on the Brooklyn Bridge. The crash into the car ahead of them and the sight of her mother, bleeding and unconscious in the front seat next to her dead father. She replayed the emotions, the longing to go back home, to get away from that place, the trip to the hospital in the ambulance with the body of her father covered with a sheet on the seat next to her; her mother taken to another hospital in a different ambulance. She wanted to go home. She was taken to her uncle's house where she waited all night to hear from anyone about her parents. No one said a thing.

"No", she thought, "I can't keep thinking about this. No one understands. No one else was there. It doesn't help to remember it. He's gone. I can't get my life back the way it was."

Grandma moved in with another daughter after Daddy died. It was a relief for Sarah not to have someone sleeping in her bed. Now she had her own room back where she could cry and not have to explain it to anyone else.

This summer, however, Grandma was back with them although not sharing Sarah's bed. She was grateful for this; what she didn't know was that Grandma was paying for the whole cottage hence she had the largest room.

"Who was she talking to?" Sarah thought it might be her Grandpa who had died when Sarah was one year old. "She never spoke to him before when she lived with us. Perhaps he was closer to her now."

The realization she might also lose her Grandma to death made her hypervigilant. She had been this was for the longest time with her mother, listening for her breathing all night long. This was especially true right after the accident when Sarah was caring for her alone.

Sometimes she thought death wasn't such a bad thing after all. She wished she had died with her father so she wouldn't have to go on living without him. He was her only friend, the only one who understood her. Her mother was such a different sort of person with so many problems of her own, Sarah hesitated to burden her with details of her own life. She didn't share the love of music or the sense of humor Sarah and Adam shared. They both saw humor in the same things in the same way. Mother tried to understand what they were laughing at together but it was impossible to explain. Mother was always so serious.

So what, there was nothing to laugh at any longer. She envied those children who still had both living parents who could smile about things, anything!

One evening while they were eating dinner the oddest thing happened. Mother had made baked potatoes. Sarah liked hers with sour cream. The fresh sour cream delivered by the local dairy farmer at the cottage was the best she had ever tasted.

Sarah heaped the sour cream on her potato and dug right in. What she didn't realize was how hot the potato was under the layer of cold sour cream. When she swallowed the first piece, it burned her esophagus, causing her heart to stop. She slumped over her plate. Her arm went into the food, burning the outside of her wrist but she had no awareness of it.

Mother and Grandma watched this and pulled her away from the table, leaning her back onto the daybed where Esther slept at night.

Sarah was travelling rapidly through a tunnel. As she looked toward a light, events from her short lifetime were presented to her like movies on a screen. Things that seemed so important in her life had very little meaning in the movie and things she thought were inconsequential suddenly assumed great importance. It didn't make any sense at all. The light became brighter and brighter. She knew she had to go in its direction.

She watched the scenes about her father. She wished she could touch him but they went by too fast. In a distance, she heard voices singing. It was the lullaby her mother sang to her when she was an infant. This time it wasn't her mother singing , it was a chorus with the sound of heavenly angels.

She travelled back in time until she found herself in her crib. Lying there, she looked at the decals her parents had placed on the sides of the crib. They were of pink and blue bunnies and lambs. Parts of the decals had peeled a bit, just as she remembered them when she was an infant.

"How cute", she thought, "they were expecting and infant. They must think I am still very small."

She remembered looking at the decals when she was an infant and thinking the same thing.

She heard a voice calling her, telling her to look to the light.

This time the light was the light from the window in her parent's bedroom which she could see from her crib.

"Wake up daughter, wake up."

The voice sounded like the narrator from her dreams telling her to wake up. She found herself back in the bungalow, a glowing man by her side. Her mother and grandmother were sitting alongside her, crying. The man told them she was all right, to give her something to eat. He left and she sat up.

Her life was changed completely after that. She knew several things as a result of that experience.

She knew she would grow up after all and not die soon. She knew there was something she had yet to do with her life. Although the purpose was made perfectly clear at the time of her visit out of time, she had no recollection of what it was when she returned to her body.

She also knew there was no such thing as time. All time was relative and perceived by us because of the limitations of our bodies and minds. She knew that time was not linear, but all time was available in another plane of existence and travel was possible to what we perceive as the past and future.

She knew she had a Savior, a being who moved in and out of time to guide her and help her understand her life. It was the same voice she heard in her dreams, the one who explained what her dreams were about and what she had to do with the information. It was the same voice she had heard from the beginning of her conscious life.

Although she was without a father in this life, she had a father who would be with her until the end of time, even after her physical life had ended. She knew there was no such thing as death.

Chapter 12
The Joy Is In The Finding (Rivka's Story)

I told them not to buy me those cones of string like they use in the bakery to wrap up the boxes. I preferred to make my doilies out of the little pieces of string they all saved for me. I'd take those pieces and undo the knots. I would then sort them by color and join the ends the way a weaver had taught me. You unwrap the ends for about an inch or so, fold them back over each other and twist the loose threads together to make one continuous string.

I would sort the strings by color. That way I'd know there they came from. Ebinger's thread was brown and white. The bakery near Miriam's house used green and white. The one on King's Highway used blue and white. Ebinger's was the most generous. I got some long pieces from them. That one girl would just wrap and wrap while she was talking adding more and more string until she shouted "Next!" to the next person in line.

Miriam and Fay said they found out where the bakeries got the cones of string that hung on the hooks from the ceiling. They would be able to buy me as many as I might want in whatever colors I'd like but I didn't want them to do that. Part of the joy in making the doilies was in the finding of the string. Part of the joy was in undoing the knots and joining the ends so they could be rolled into balls.

In the Depression, when a sweater would get worn out, I would unravel it and use whatever good yarn I could salvage to make up a new sweater, adding it to other unraveled yarn from other worn sweaters to make up the difference in the yardage. I'd do the same with other garments, using what wasn't worn, cutting them up and making new things out of old. I learned to make patterns out of brown paper bags, measuring the clothes that fit and copying their outlines onto the paper, giving a little allowance for the seams.

Imagine, I was a privileged girl in Russia who had servants in my home to do such work. I went to a private Gymnasium. I never knew how to sew a stitch or cook a meal until I married Mordechai and we no longer had any servants. I had to learn everything .

When we went to America things got even worse. We lived in crowded tenements until Mordechai was assigned to a synagogue in Massachusettes. We lived in a small house there. It was there that the children got Scarlet Fever and Esther was sent out to a hospital for six weeks to treat her kidney failure.

It was like when I had Typhus back home. I was so sick I thought I would die for certain. My fever was so high, I went into a coma. While I was in the coma, I went underground on a sled. Down in the earth I travelled through piles of buried bodies wrapped like mummies, like cocoons. The stench of that place! I was sick but I could not move. A man stood at the end of the underground tunnel. He was surrounded with light like an angel. He told me that I had to go back, that it wasn't time for me to be there. I woke from the coma. The fever had passed.

Whoever said life in America would be easy? I watched my baby die from dysentery. I waited for my son to come home from Midway Island where he had been stationed as a cook in the army. He wasn't even in combat and he was missing in action. I knew he was dead but I never lost hope I might have been wrong, that he was alive somewhere and would one day return to us. I saw my daughter's spouses die and I knew my oldest daughter had died, too even if they wouldn't tell me so. They wanted to spare me. I was very old.

They always wanted to spare me. It didn't help. I felt alone, uninvolved in the events of my family. My deafness isolated me enough. I didn't need to be protected from reality be well-meaning children.

As deaf as I was, I did know when they were talking about me.

They said I must have some sort of radar, that I tuned in when they whispered or mentioned my name. Truth is, I could hear better than they thought, especially when they didn't shout at me; but I could not understand a lot of the things they said. They spoke a different language.

They talked about modern things, things we did not talk about in my generation. They talked about people's troubles, their operations and illnesses. Always there was a scandal somewhere! All they had to do to find one was to look in their own lives but they never did. It was always someone else's misfortune they discussed.

What were they saying about me? That I was getting old? That I was slowing down, forgetting things, losing interest in things I used to enjoy? All I wanted to do was rest. Raising nine children to adulthood was a lot of work.

It was my time to take it easy now and make the doilies out of the bakery string. They didn't have to use them! It was something to keep my hands occupied so I didn't feel so useless. My hands shook when I tried to do anything other than crochet. When I carried my cup to my lip, my hands shook so I often broke the cup when placing it on the saucer. I embarrassed them with the shaking and my deafness and my accent and how I looked and how I dressed and my old-fashioned ideas.

I spoiled Miriam's perfect house and I was in the way at Fay's although she would never say so. Rachel had so many problems of her own I dared not intrude in her life. Sam, my only living son was an idiot, a big disappointment; but if I told him that to his face, he would turn it right back to me so I kept my mouth shut. Dotty was so crazy she often didn't know anyone else was in the house when I came to visit. It was good to be ignored by her. Lydia, my baby, my albatross! How can I explain her? She was a good person who made bad choices. Whenever she did, it was my fault. I accepted the blame as she couldn't. Pauline died before I did. I wasn't supposed to know. Her husband had died several years before but not without causing a lot of grief and sadness due to his dementia.

Then there was Esther; always coming up short in her life. What did she want? "To be like everyone else." She wasn't. I always felt bad that she didn't know her father until she was over a year old. He was waiting for us on the dock in New York Harbor as he had come to America before us, paving the way as it were. Esther was my last European baby.

I treasured my last European baby and wished things might have been different in our lives. She loved her father so much. She was so much like him. If only she could cry and show emotion. Sometimes I felt there were two of her, one who lived with us and one who appeared to the rest of the world.

After Mordechai died I lived with Lydia and the baby. If he were still alive, she would have had to give this baby up as she had done with the first one. It was hard enough for her to give up the first one; but Mordechai was adamant that no daughter of his would raise a child without a proper marriage. As the father of the baby did not follow the Jewish religion and had no intention of converting, marriage in the synagogue was out of the question. I devoted my energy to helping her raise her son. It took my mind off the sadness of losing my husband of fifty years.

This next generation of my grandchildren was different or was it me who was different? They were Americans. They spoke English as their first language. They were born after the Depression, most of them after World War II. They didn't know want or hardship or fear.

Fay's daughter Sheryl was the same age as Lydia. They were more like cousins than aunt and niece. When Fay was widowed, it wasn't much longer before her daughter Sheryl was widowed, too. It all happened around the same time. Steve, Herschel, Mike, Pauline, Adam, all died, all before the age of sixty. It's funny how we didn't think that was so unusual then. It was living to an old age that was unusual. I was unusual. I was eighty-six when I died.

I died of boredom. I was tired of living. I was tired of people telling me how old I was and wondering how much longer I would live. There was nothing physically wrong with me. There was a time when I was younger when my life was in danger. That was when I was having children one after another and the doctor told me another pregnancy might cost me my life. I had five more pregnancies after that. I had no choice, we were observant Jews, not permitted to use any type of birth- control . Then, of course, was the time I had Typhus; but you have already heard about that.

I was tired of not being able to hear what was on TV. I turned the dial up so far it was at the end and still I couldn't hear it. I knew it was very loud but all I could hear was a rumble, no words. The people who spoke Yiddish were dying, too so I had few people to speak with comfortably. The ones who lived in Esther's neighborhood were laughable. When they heard me speak with my enormous accent, they asked if I was American-born. Can you believe that?

I would read my Yiddish-language paper, "The Forward", and try to tell my family about the news in the paper which they told me they had already heard on TV or the radio. When I lived with Esther and my granddaughter, Sarah, Esther had a way of interpreting the news which was different from most other people. I suppose you could say she was a little paranoid . That was understandable given the uncertainty of her world which began early in her life.

She hated that I would play the TV so loud. I knew her time would come when she would do the same thing. Too bad she didn't know how loud it was when she did it too!

When we went to the Catskills for a vacation, Esther, Sarah and I, the strangest thing happened. I began to hear voices. I thought it was a part of the deafness, that I heard sounds that weren't really there, simply imagined in my mind. I figured if I imagined them, they didn't have much to tell me that I didn't know. That was not the case. They did tell me things I didn't know to prepare me for my last voyage. Often sitting in that big dark room in the bungalow, the one with dark wood paneling on the walls, I would think I was back on the ship that brought us here so long ago. I would go back to thinking I had the little ones with me and I had to keep them from being frightened and sick.

I would drift off to sleep and dream about things I couldn't tell anyone about.

Sarah had that gift, the gift of dreams. I knew it when she was a little child and she would tell her mother about her voyages at night. She didn't know this but it was an old Russian custom to start the day by discussing the dreams of the previous night. It helped start things that way by trying to unravel the meaning of the dreams. Perhaps the waking hours would flow more easily, linking them to the messages of the dreams.

It was the dreams that weren't discussed that were disturbing. Those were ones that would have benefitted from discussion.

What is death but a time when the spirit leaves the body permanently and does not return at the end of the dream? Each night I'd close my eyes, hoping it would be the time it would last forever. It didn't happen when we were in the bungalow although Sarah nearly died then. It happened later when I was living in the nursing home. I thought it was a kindness that one of my family members did not have to find my lifeless body, that it was the nursing home staff that did. It didn't matter much anyway, I hadn't been using it a lot, spending most of my time outside of it, hoping not to have to go back in. If the string was severed, the one that brought the spirit back into the body after a dream voyage was over the life would be over, too.

What total joy in finding I was free at last! The last piece of the bakery string was cut. I could move on. "Next"! I thought of the girl at Ebinger's as she tore the string from the cone and I kept on going without the burden of my body.

"She died of loneliness" they all murmured at my funeral. They felt guilty for leaving me in the nursing home.

"I died of boredom!" I shouted but they didn't hear me.

Chapter 13
If We Have No Past We Have No Future (Pescha's first story)

"Give me that shirt and I'll turn the collar for you. It's looking very worn."

" I think you already turned the collar on this shirt, Ma."

"You're right, Elie, I did. Leave it in the basket and I'll put a new one on for you."

Pescha sat in the sitting room with a pile of mending in a basket on the table. She was going through the work methodically a piece at a time as she did every weekday evening at this time.

Mr. Kozlofsky, the boarder, was sitting in his chair, smoking a cigar and reading his newspaper as Pescha sewed, humming softly to herself.

The children were at the kitchen table, working on their homework, their father was in front in the store doing the inventory and balancing the books.

From where Pescha sat, she could see them all except for Sam, her husband. It was a quiet evening, warm enough to have the windows open so she could hear the bustle of the noisy street below and the clatter of the elevated train as it rounded the turn on its way to Coney Island.

"How did we get her?" she thought as she sewed. "Was it really so bad in Odessa that we had to come here?"

Her whole family had come over within several years. They were among the first wave of immigrants to come to this place. Trouble was brewing in Odessa, trouble over the whole Ukraine in fact. They were Russians, too, even though they were Jews. They knew no other place than Odessa. Was there any other place worth mentioning? Odessa was the center of the world. There were rumors of Communism, rumors of the overthrow of the Tsar. The Tsar was very anti-Semitic but rumor had it that the Communists would be worse. Rumor had it that what the Tsar's army didn't destroy in their villages would be destroyed by the Communist revolution and life would be even harder. The Communists were against all religion, "the opiate of the people" they called it. Religion kept the people oppressed so they would not revolt against the corrupt regime. The priests of the church manipulated the Royals to gain power. It was time for that to end.

All that had passed long ago. Now Russia was a communist country. The Tsar and his whole family were killed savagely by the revolutionaries. Pescha was not particularly enamored with the Tsar; but what the Communists did was so horrible, so inhuman! Even those little girls, the daughters killed and the little boy, Alexander, the one with the blood disease, he was dead, too.

Maybe they were right, it was better here. Didn't they have a nice business and a nice place to live big enough to take in boarders to help pay the rent? Maybe one day they would own that building once they were better able to understand the laws of property transfer in America.

Pescha saved her money. She had brought some jewelry with her from Russia and she kept it in a safe place in the house. No one knew where it was except for her and Sam. It was their emergency resource, not to be used unless they absolutely had no other way to survive. They could take so little with them on the boat that brought them here. She was able to bring a few things that had sentimental value, among them a crocheted bedspread from her trousseau and some embroidered linens she made for the table. She had sewn almost everything they wore and knew how to repair those garments to get the most out of them. She was so far from home. Thoughts of her parents and in-laws kept coming to mind. They were long gone. Would she and Sam have made this long trip if their parents were alive? She doubted it. Family was a strong tie. They would have stayed where they were. She knew the older people would never leave Odessa and venture into the New World.

She took comfort in knowing her sister and brother were with them in Brooklyn. Her sister, whom no one would believe was her sister had white hair. It was inherited by some members of the family. As black as Pescha's hair was, that's how white Manya's was in contrast. It had turned white before she reached her thirtieth birthday. Her brother, too, had white hair. It made him look distinguished although he was just as childish as he could be under that head of white hair.

They were starting to adjust, all of them, to America. The dreams of streets paved with gold were only dreams. They were a minority in the country although they were a majority in the neighborhoods they settled in. Sometimes when she listened to the sounds of the voices of the people in the street on Brighton Beach Avenue, she would think she was still in Odessa. There were so many people living there from home!

"Being in America surely didn't change any of them", she remarked on evening at the dinner table," they are still wheeling and dealing as they did back home. Every time Mrs. Schachter comes into the store she sends her little Louie to pick out what he wants from the candy jars. While I am watching him, she helps herself to something off a shelf and puts it in her pocket. She thinks I don't see her do it. How smart she is, like her husband the greengrocer who charges a little extra because his scale is not set on zero. You can take them out of the Old Country but you can't take the Old Country out of them."

Salesmen came to the store bringing their stocks of candy and school supplies from warehouses in the city. Pescha and Sam were tied to the store. They couldn't go to the warehouses themselves to buy the goods. The store was open six days a week, closed only on Saturday, the Sabbath.

With the salesmen came tales of the way other people lived in the city of New York.

"You wouldn't believe what I saw! I saw a man dressed as a woman walking down a street in the Theater District just as plain as day. He had no shame, this man. I said in Yiddish, 'What a disgrace you are to your family', but he didn't understand me. It's better he didn't.

"I see rich people every day. You can't imagine how rich they are, all of them Gentiles. The Gentiles own New York City and the politicians run it. They hate the Jews but we do all the business. Who do you think makes all the clothes the rich people wear? We do. We make them in sweat shops on the Lower East Side. People take work home with them called 'piece work'. They get paid by the piece for each thing they make. They live in tenements, several families in one cold-water flat and everyone is sewing all the time, even the little children. The children don't go to school, they are needed to sew. As long as the parents don't register them for school, no one knows they should be there. When the truant officer comes to the tenement to see how many children live there, they are hidden away.

Can you imagine? The fine people who buy these clothes and paying good money for them, too, do you think they know who is making them and how much they are getting paid and who is getting richer off them? There is talk of labor unions and all kinds of child labor laws. How can they do this to us? Where will we get money to live? How can they take away the work from the children and send them to school where they will learn more subversive things?"

The salesman went on talking about the political scene, all filtered through his survival instinct and his minimal command of English. Then he told him more about the rest of the world, the places outside the city where the immigrants lived.

"There are farms up north of the city and big fancy houses. That's where the rich people live. They don't want to come down here and mingle with the crowds in the city. They send their servants there to do the shopping. The men work in those big office buildings during the day, shielded from the crowds below. They go back to their mansions up north of the city at night and don't think about what is happening under their noses. They are angry we came here. They don't like immigrants. This is their country, they say, they settled it. We are dirty and ignorant and should go back to Europe where we came from."

Pescha knew about prejudice. She also knew about God and God's will. If it was God's will they move to America to start a new life, that's what they would do. Education was the key. The children would learn to read and write English .They would have what their parents did not. They would have freedom.

There was no dictator here, no Tsar. Even if they were ridiculed for being "Greenhorns" and Jews, their children and grandchildren would live in a free country where every man had the same chance to learn, succeed, to worship as he chose. If one worked hard enough and saved his money, he could have a comfortable life in America and no one could take it away from him. No one would be burning his synagogue or his village.

There were a lot of ideas being talked about: a lot of new thinking being done. The Communist Party set up shop on the boardwalk of Brighton Beach. The old men who were running away from the Tsar in Russia were now members of the Communist Party in America. Even Leon Trotsky was in America, living in the Bronx. What was he doing here? Was he waiting for the revolution to be over so he could return to the bliss of the workers' state?

"That's why we're here", she thought, "in America where everyone is free to express himself, free to speak, to learn, to succeed. In Russia if you were born into a poor family, you had no hope of being anything but poor.

That's why there were so many fairy tales about paupers and princes changing places and magic beings who granted wishes of those who had no other hope to improve their lives. The streets may not be paved with gold, like we were told, but there is a chance for even the poorest to be successful."

She looked fondly at her children. Elie was her favorite boy. His American name was Adam, but at home he was called Elie. He was the third oldest, the first one born in America. He became very ill when he was little with Diphtheria and it damaged his heart. The doctor said it was life-threatening and he might not live very long, although here he was, fourteen years old and although he was small, he was growing up. He was offered the opportunity to go to a camp in the summer. The camp was in the Adirondacks, far from Brooklyn. She thought it would do him some good so she agreed to let him go. When the school year would end he would be off to camp with some other children from the city. No matter how far away the camp was, it was nowhere near as far as Russia.

Often she would go down to the boardwalk to sit and look at the ocean that divided the Old World from the New; "Columbus' medine" "Columbus' goldine medine", that is, the golden land of promise. The world was changing so fast. There were so many things happening in her own neighborhood. Thank God for the children to explain what was going on in the larger world. Thank God for the children to help her when her English failed her.

For generations, in Odessa , her family had lived in the same place, doing the same business with the same people day after day. Every day was the same. She longed for that boring predictable sameness and tried to reproduce it in her life in America. Holidays, Sabbaths, rituals; she clung to their patterns to get her bearings in this odd place. She tried to tell the children about what Odessa was like though they were more interested in what was new in Brooklyn. There were moving pictures they wanted to see and programs on the radio they liked to hear. There were cousins and friends who wanted to take the subway into New York City and see the sights there. There was a world beyond Brighton Beach Avenue and six days a week at the family store. There was a world accessible to anyone who had a penny to ride the train.

Chapter 14
The Reports of My Dementia
(Pescha's Second Story)

The reports of my dementia have been greatly exaggerated, I am pleased to say. For those of you who knew me on Earth, I am sorry for having caused you so much displeasure. The dementia now is a thing of the past, a thing long past, I am happy to report to my friends and family.

For those who may be my descendents, I can assure you it is not hereditary. Any mental problem you may develop in your lives is not in any way a result of the transmission of my genetic material. Though I can't be responsible for any other hereditary units you might introduce.

Dementia can be a frightening thing for your loved ones to witness; but here's the good news, the demented person doesn't know a thing about it. "A thing about what?" (It's an old dementia joke, humor me).

You see, I had a sense of humor after all! You have to have one to survive. Adam (Elie) and I used to joke about things all the time. Leah was so weepy, you couldn't be funny with her or she would burst out crying. I think that girl cried every day of her life when she was growing up.

I'm glad Adam was the one to help me out after my husband, Samuel died. Morris was too involved with his fancy wife and child. Herman had potential to go far in his education and needed to continue in school, but Adam was still a boy, only fifteen years old. Apart from being sickly, Adam was very helpful in the store. He was also very quick to take up the role of his younger sister Leah's protector.

Adam had a knack for giving humorous names to people he was fond of, or who had a distinguishing characteristic. It was a way to remember them for him. A lot of people didn't understand or appreciate the creativity of Adam's "pet" names but I loved them. They even helped me with my English, they were so descriptive. What am I talking about? For example: Leah was dubbed "Flower-Pot-Head". This was because after she washed her thick, curly hair, it was totally unmanageable and stood away from her head like an unruly bouquet of flowers. Those names always stuck. It was a family tradition. I did it myself when I was a girl. Come to think of it, isn't that the way people acquired their last names in the very old days?

For me, a picture really is worth a thousand words. I am a visual person. That is why it was such a tragedy when my vision became clouded over with the cataracts. I struggled with them for years before I would agree to have them removed. Even then, it was a difficult recovery, having to wear those awful dark glasses and still not being able to see very well.

When Leah's time came to have her cataracts removed, it was a procedure completed in one day with a lens implanted that corrected her vision immediately. She was so happy with the first procedure, she had the other eye done within the month.

As I told you, the dementia is not genetic. The cataracts are.

Adam and Herman didn't live long enough to develop them. Leah did. If Morris had them, I think he chose to keep them as seeing well wasn't that important to him. Anyone who rode in a car when he was driving would attest to that.

My greatest passion in life ever since I was a little girl was needlework. I loved to sew and embroider designs on the fabrics I sewed into garments. I loved also to knit and crochet. I would liked to have done more knitting; but crochet worked up so much faster and speed was important when the items you make are to be worn or used in the home. Later on, when my eyesight began to fail, I did a lot more knitting as you didn't have to look at it, you could feel the stitches as you went along.

Many people do not know this about me that I would have loved to have learned how to draw and paint. Drawing was not something encouraged in our culture; in fact it was forbidden, just like acting or singing anything other than the liturgy. We were also forbidden to adorn ourselves with makeup or jewelry. If I had lived in another time I might have been an artist but I learned to express my art in my needlework, like the Amish who make colorful quilts while bright colors and designs are forbidden in their own dress.

Living in Odessa, I felt like I was living in the center of the world. There were people moving through that city from everywhere, East and West. Walking down those streets one might hear languages from all over Europe and North Africa as well as Central Asia and even the Far East. Along with many languages there were the varieties of dress, foodstuffs and treasures these merchants brought to trade and sell. It was as if Odessa was a ship that travelled around the world except the world came to Odessa.

When the troubles became more intense, my husband said we would be leaving Odessa. He knew of a place in America that was so much like it, I wouldn't miss it quite so much. He was right. Brighton Beach even looked like Odessa, although there I was the stranger travelling from another place.

It was easier to learn English working in the store. People came in all the time and often there was no way out of it. If they didn't speak Yiddish or Russian and none of the children were there to help, I'd have to speak English. The children were a great help teaching me and their father English words and expressions they learned at school.

I am told that now there are many Russians in Brighton Beach who don't bother to learn English. Even the signs on the businesses are written in Russian. I suppose a person could be a merchant there now and never speak one word of English! That's fine for them but how would I have been able to speak to my grandchildren? They would speak English. They are Americans.

My husband, Samuel, was a kind man. He would never say anything unkind to or about anyone. He was quiet and small in stature. The trip to America and the acclimation to the new culture were difficult for him. The pace of life was fast and he had to work long hours to keep the business going. I was busy with the children so I couldn't help him so much when they were small. When they went to school, I could spend more time in the store. By then, his health was beginning to decline. Soon, I was alone with the children trying to make ends meet. I had to take in sewing in addition to the work in the candy store. I used to love to sew. That was when it was something I did not have to do to survive. It's funny how when a hobby becomes your source of income, it's no longer a hobby. It's work.

My daughter-in-law, Esther used to be very hard on me. She would say I had a lot of money put away. It was her opinion that money was not to be saved but spent. I suppose that's why her family always had money problems. We had a little money. We were not rich by any stretch of the imagination but we were able to get through the Depression and keep the business open.

Leah got a good job after she finished high school. She worked for a lawyer as a legal secretary. Nowadays, that job is called "Paralegal" and pays a whole lot more. I was proud of her that she could have such an important job. Too bad her love life didn't go as well. Then again, I don't know. She loved children and was not able to have any but how would she have been as a parent? She was very loving but so emotional I don't think a child of hers would have been able to ever leave her house. She was so worried about everything. I suppose it was my fault in a way. She was my only daughter. She lost her father at such a young age. I took care to shield her from harm. What would she do without me to help her? I should have thought more about that and been a little more strict about her learning to take care of herself and be a homemaker.

I thought working in the business world would expose her to more life situations, but it didn't. All it exposed her to was a lot of legal terminology and a lot of typing.

I tried to get her interested in the things that interested me as a girl, but she was so different. I got her a piano and started her with lessons but Adam was the one who learned how to play. I tried to teach her to sew and do needle crafts but she refused to learn, thinking that was what caused me to lose my vision. I tried to explain that that had nothing to do with it, though it was useless once she started to cry.

Esther was very jealous of the relationship I had with Leah. She would make fun of us, being so close. She wasn't very close to her own mother so she couldn't understand how a grown woman would prefer the company of her own female parent over someone her own age.

In my family, people talk about things. We make jokes about life. We find ways to help as a family when someone has a problem. This was unusual to Esther, she expected Adam to leave all of his family behind him when he married her and care only for her. She tried but she couldn't keep Leah from visiting them after I died. She couldn't even keep Leah from visiting after Adam died.

I recall a visit when I was in the nursing home near the Ocean Parkway Jewish Center. Esther walked over with my year-old granddaughter, Sarah. I wished I could have told her how much I enjoyed seeing that little one. The little girl was so much like Adam, her father, when he was that age. Adam was so much like me! If I wasn't so demented and she wasn't so young , I might have been able to develop some rapport with her.

I'm so happy when Leah was cleaning out her place before she moved to Florida that she sent those old photographs of me to Sarah. We looked exactly alike at the same age. She's a lot like me in many ways and so are her children.

I would like to reassure them again that the dementia is not inherited; at least not from my side of the family.

I would also like them to know that Leah, Esther and I are doing very nicely here. We get along just fine now that we have gotten away from that stuffy laboratory known as life on Earth.

Chapter 15
Leah's Story

I was the last one born in my family and the only girl. My three brothers were the loves of my life. I never wanted to be like them, however as they were boys and I was special, I was a girl.

Mama wanted a girl so badly she risked her life to have me. She had diabetes and pregnancy was very risky in those days if you were diabetic and had high blood pressure, too. I was a very big baby because of Mama's diabetes but this was not well understood. People thought I was healthy because I was born so big but that was not true.

I was given every privilege my parents could afford to give me. I was offered music lessons at a young age. I was not very good at the piano. Adam learned more at my lessons than I did. He hid behind a curtain and listened to everything the teacher said. He used to tease me because I got the lessons and he didn't but he knew enough not to come out from behind the curtain. If Adam had asked for lessons, he would have been denied them. They were a luxury not needed by someone who would be taking over the family business.

Mama loved to sew pretty clothes for me. She made all my outfits even after I was grown. She was a seamstress, you know. Embroidery was her specialty, even after she developed cataracts. I never wanted to learn any of her skills. I was afraid I would not be able to do them as well as she did. She was a perfectionist. If a pattern wasn't coming out right in her estimation, she would rip it out again and again until she got it the way she wanted. Reading the directions in English was always a challenge for her. Mostly, she would look at the pictures to understand how the stitches went. I would try to help her as best I could but I didn't have the experience with the actual craft and the terminology.

I was an excellent student at school. I loved to please people and pleasing my teachers made me feel important. I studied stenography in high school and loved it. It was like a secret code. No one knew what I was writing and I could pass notes to my friends who also knew stenography. I became a legal secretary when I graduated from school. I loved my job for I got to meet lots of interesting people and learn all their legal secrets. I was as smart as the lawyer I worked for and he often would let me make up briefs on my own. He would proofread them and sign them. I had a lot of responsibility in the office with none of the headaches as I was only a secretary.

Life was interesting. I had a steady boyfriend, a job and a nice home. My mother took care of me and I took care of her. She was a loving person who never said an unkind word about anyone. As her vision began to fail she could no longer take in sewing. By then I was able to support both of us. I had a lot of nice things, including several fur coats. I went to night school to study singing which was a rewarding hobby. Later on, I worked at the USO to entertain soldiers who came back to the states. I would never ever consider going overseas to do that. Mama would never allow it. My boyfriend was drafted so I had no one to spend time with. Sometimes I'd go to the USO just to see if he was sent back for a while. Eventually, so much time passed, the war ended and I never heard from him again.

Things were getting bad with Mama. Her mind was deteriorating rapidly from hardening of the arteries to her brain. She couldn't be left alone, she was confused and frightened. Sometimes she would say things that upset people, especially Esther, but she really didn't mean them. She had no control over that any longer. Esther had a lot of ideas as to what to do to make Mama feel better. She suggested taking her away for a vacation somewhere. She didn't understand that the worst thing I could have done would be to take her away from familiar surroundings. Mama was confused as it was at home. Taking her away from her home would have been devastating.

People asked me if I had a new love interest after the War. How could I? There was Mama and there was work and that was enough to keep me busy. When Mama died, I met Harry. He was a good man, quite a bit older than I but reliable and with no obligations. When you get to be in your late thirties, the men you meet usually have children and lots of history. Although I loved children dearly, I would not have been a good mother to someone else's children. I was too much of a spoiler and too set in my own ways.

When I married Harry, my nieces and nephews attended the wedding. I paid for the wedding myself. Everyone had a great time, especially my brothers who were relieved I was no longer an old maid. Harry and I had a good life together even though he was very cheap and self-centered. He planned to move to Florida after he retired but he worked until the day he died. I moved to Florida and spent my remaining years and his money there without him. I did manage to save some money to give to my nieces and nephews.

Always a romantic, I liked to help young people with their romances and loved to hear their love stories. Life for me was a storybook, full of romance and fantasy. I guess I never really got over Manny, my first real boyfriend (or gentleman friend as they used to say). He was so sweet to me, always bringing me presents. My brothers hated him, especially Adam who was sure he was up to no good. Nothing happened between us, ever. That's because Manny was gay.

They didn't call it that, then. He went into the Army to prove he was a man. It didn't matter to me. I loved him the way he was. He was safe. Some people joked that he was prettier than I was and I suppose he was. I was more earthy and he more ethereal. We complemented each other.

Mama was sure I would not be able to survive without her. She had always done everything for me. I never wanted to learn things most girls did. I hated to cook and sew. Oh, I liked playing house with dolls. I wanted to remain a child forever. My childhood was taken away from me when my Papa died. I was eleven years old. Even though I was an adult physically I wanted to remain a child forever. Nine is early to start menstruating and I didn't understand what that was until I was a teenager. My girlfriends started much later and made a big fuss about it. What's the big deal? I had been doing that for years.

Sure, I wanted babies but that never happened. I had to have surgery when I was thirty-five for a cyst on my ovary. They took the ovary out and I felt like a pariah afterward. Etta, my brother Morris' wife made a big fuss about it saying I was deformed and would never be "right" again.

Esther was certain I was having an abortion when I went for that surgery. How could that be? It was right about the time Sarah was born and Sarah later fantasized that I was her real mother and gave her up for adoption. I wish that were true, too but Sarah really was Esther's child.

Of all the nieces and nephews I felt closest to Sarah. She was the most like me. Her Daddy died when she was twelve. I loved my brother Adam so much. He was the one at home with me and Mama for the longest time until he married Esther. She thought I didn't like her. I did like her although she was difficult to get along with. Her family was different from ours, each one so suspicious of the others at all times. Mama loved us all and didn't play favorites. We didn't fight amongst ourselves like Esther's family. Everyone knew the boys were the favorites there.

I wasn't too thrilled with Morris' wife but she was a schoolteacher and knew more than I did about everything. Herman's wife was a sweetheart. She loved everyone and they loved her back. She was a good mother, too to my nephews.

I spent a lot of time with Sarah . I liked to bring her activity books and craft kits. I enjoyed playing with those as much as she did. Sarah looked so much like Mama it was frightening. I liked to be around her just to look at her face. She was so much like Mama but I didn't know Mama when she was a young girl. The older Sarah got the more she looked like Mama as I remembered her except Sarah was very tall and Mama was short, like me.

It's funny, in our family we all look so much alike it's as if no one else carries any genes along but us. Even Sarah's first son, Adam looked exactly like her father, the man he was named for. We joke about it, saying one could always pick out the Gilberts in a crowd. I never did get to see Sarah's younger children but I have seen pictures and I know her youngest daughter looks exactly like me! They even call her "Little Leah."

They all know it now. Our family legacy is depression. No, not "The Depression", depression, like feeling sad all the time. Some of them take medication for it. I never did. I'd rather have a good cry and get it out in the open. I certainly cried a lot in my lifetime. I also worried a lot. "About what?" I worried about everything. I don't know why. It didn't do any good to worry that much, things worked out any way. I only wanted them to know I cared about them when I said I was worried. It was my way of staying connected if you know what I mean.

I was sick for so many years with high blood pressure and arthritis and depression that my final illness came as a big surprise. Can you believe it? I died from bleeding to death from somewhere in my gastro-intestinal tract. It was a strange thing. I had no pain or discomfort, simply a gradual weakening and then, death. The first thing Sarah said when she heard how I died was that I must have been taking medication for the arthritis that caused the bleeding. I wasn't. She should have known better than that. I would never take any medication the doctors would give me for any reason. Their medications were always too strong for me. Mama taught me that. I was a delicate person and could not tolerate normal doses of anything.

After all those years of worrying, you would have thought I'd have gotten an ulcer a long time ago. When a person worries and cries all the time an ulcer doesn't form. It's only when they hold the sadness inside that an ulcer starts. I never held it in.

No one knows how or when the bleeding started. The autopsy didn't reveal much about the cause. It was a peaceful way to go and I'm glad I did not go to the hospital until the very last minute when there was nothing to be done for me. They found me in my room, dead, when they came to take me for a test. What a relief that was. No more tests!

I was eighty-one when I died. I had a good life except at the end I had a lot of trouble getting around because of my arthritis. I didn't want to use a wheelchair so I stayed by myself in my apartment. So many of my Florida friends were sick and dying, I was finally glad to get out of there.

It was hard for my nephews to go to my place and pack things up. They felt bad they hadn't seen me before I died. What was there to see? Now I know worrying doesn't help. When you tell someone you are worried about them it makes them feel bad, as thought they were in some danger they were not aware of. There is no real danger and nothing to fear, not even death. It came so quickly for me I had no time to fear. The good news is that I didn't have to clean my apartment before I left! All my things were taken care of by my nephews. Thanks and God bless you. I mean that with all my heart.

Chapter 16
Uncharted Territory

High school: A new world. Neither of Sarah's parents had continued in school beyond the eighth grade. Sarah was now in the tenth grade, out of junior high school into Erasmus Hall High School at last.

Junior high had been so difficult. Although a good student, Sarah suffered from the loss of her father. She was truly on her own when she began seventh grade. Mathematics had always been hard for her and her ninth grade teacher was less than helpful. She had to ask a neighbor to tutor her to pass the course.

High school geometry was a great surprise. She loved it and regained confidence in her ability to learn mathematics once again. Biology, geometry, English, French, history; all were exciting. Erasmus Hall High School or EHHS as it was known to its students was an oasis of learning within the busy city streets of Flatbush, Church and Bedford Avenues. The original school was a private school for boys built by the Dutch Reformed Church in the eighteenth century. The public high school was built around the little wooden building of the original school and was laid out in the form of a quadrangle of four imposing Gothic stone edifices. The structure of the school made it look like a castle complete with gargoyles and beautiful stone arches. When city children walked through those arches on Flatbush or Bedford Avenues, they entered a new world, a world of learning and new challenges. Dedicated teachers brought the best of their disciplines to eager young minds. Their class was one of the largest ever to attend that school, but they were used to the crowding and the split sessions as their class was always the largest wherever they went. They were early baby-boomers, born right after the end of World War II.

Sarah had gone to school with many of the same people since kindergarten and many were with her in high school and college as well. There were also new people to meet as more elementary schools fed into the high school. Friendships made in that school have lasted for decades. "So sad," Sarah thought," this school might be closing soon. We'll have our memories of the time that was the best in our lives although we didn't believe it then."

Who could have anticipated the characters Sarah would meet at EHHS?

A girl who shall be called "Red" walked those hallowed halls daily with the rest of the kids. She looked like she had stepped off the cover of "True Detective" magazine. Here was a woman with perfectly teased and coiffed hair in a French Twist, set with enough hairspray to fix a fly for eternity. Her lips and finger nails were fire-engine red and she wore high heels and sheer stockings with black seams every school day. Did she know the forties were over? Did she know the fifties had also passed? This was the "sixties", for heaven's sake! This was the decade of president JFK and everyone who was in school the day of his assassination heard the news on the school intercom that fateful afternoon.

It's surely no accomplishment for a teenage girl to produce fantasies in the minds of teenage boys. This girl named Red produced fantasies in the minds of teenage girls as well.

Where did she come from? What decade? What planet? Where did she return to each night when classes were over? What was her family like? What were her plans for the future? The yearbook said, "Plans to go into business". Ha. We knew what business that would be or did we?

Was she an adult secret agent sent to invade and examine the world of high school students? She wasn't under very good cover, was she?

Sarah had a cadre of friends. They were girls whose fathers had died or were absent in some other way. The girls dressed alike in order to be different as is the cardinal rule of adolescence. They wore black clothes and white lipstick, black eyeliner and lots of dark eye shadow to look "beat" and hung around the fountain in Washington Square Park with their arty friends who played guitar and sang blues and folk songs. They were easily distinguished from the "other" girls who dressed alike to be different who wore plaid pleated skirts and button-down collared blouses with knee socks and circle pins; the "preppies".

Her friends were good students who would sometimes "go underground" to hang out with the not-so-good students for fun. After all, being a nerd was not and would never be "cool".

Let's get back to Red. She was a commercial student which meant she took business courses as opposed to the academic track. The business department was just as challenging scholastically as the academic ; but the students in that track were not planning on going to college. Business was the preferred course Esther would have liked Sarah to pursue. Sarah's adolescent rebellion consisted of taking the academic path.

Sarah daydreamed about Red as their lives progressed. What was she doing at twenty? At forty? What was her life like? Sarah knew what her own life was like, the predictable life of a physician who was also the mother of children, moving from one life crisis to another as the years rolled by. But Red? Here we see her at age twenty-five, living in a trailer in the middle of a busy commercial street. Never having married, she entertained a series of older men in her life who have treated her like a woman without a brain. They bought her pretty things so she would look nice when they took her to gangland gatherings. Maybe they would rub her shellacked head for luck as they gambled away their stolen money.

Now, they are back, sitting in the trailer. He's smoking a stinky cigar. He's dressed casually in his white wife-beater undershirt, reading the racing form. One of her "Photoplay" magazines rests under his hairy elbow. She asks him to hand her the magazine. He tosses it in the trash.

"Hey, that's mine!"

"Garbage belongs in the garbage."

"Hop in, mister"

"Don't talk to me like that, girlie."

"This is my place, if you don't like it, you can leave."

(Sound of a screen door slamming)

"Good riddance, bad news."

A decade or two later, still living in the trailer, she steps outside to go shopping at the local Woolworth's for some cosmetics where she is seen frantically searching through the bins of nail polish for her signature shade, "Candy Apple Red". They don't make it any longer. They stopped making it in the sixties. Fortunately, she had amassed such a huge number of bottles back then when it was being discontinued and no one else had any need of them, she had enough to last until this time.

Red asks the manager if they have any left in the back of the store. She is taken to the storeroom to look through the dusty bins. Not everyone has this privilege. She knows the manager. He is an old friend.

Next stop, the hosiery counter: Try to find seamed stockings! If they lasted longer, she would get those expensive ones from Frederick's of Hollywood; but a working girl has to save her money.

She has been a subscriber to "Photoplay" for a long time and has amassed a large collection. The resale price of these relics when she takes them to antiques dealers will allow her to live comfortably in Florida; that and her collection of Betty Boop memorabilia in the original boxes.

Fast forward to the next century, the twenty-first: Developers want her to move her trailer so they might put up a new office building complex in her once seedy neighborhood which has now become gentrified. It is in the way even though it only takes up twenty feet of street frontage. They offer a nice price and she moves it to a trailer park in Delray Beach.

Florida is boring. Most of the men who would be interested in a "dame" like her are underground. Really. The younger ones are not interested until they learn how much money she has. Suddenly she becomes more desirable and the darling of the gay men's circle, sort of an aging star without any particular talent,

Red had committed to memory the contents of her "Photoplay" collection and had become an authority on the lives of movie stars of the '50's and '60's. Since most of them are underground as well, she can convince people she once knew those stars and begins to write fictional stories of her encounters with them. Not all of this is untrue, she had seen some of them as she passed them on the way to the ladies' room in night clubs when out on the town with her Mafia friends; but "who wants to know?"

The stories are good, based on the annals of "Photoplay" and her books become best sellers. She becomes a celebrity in her own right.

Onward to the future: Her signature style has returned. Everything retro is new again. She is sitting on top of the world. With a touch of plastic surgery she looks as good as she did in high school when she looked twenty years older than her real age. She doesn't move quite so fast on those spike heels since her hip replacements and the "Miracle Ears" sometimes make a high-pitched whistle in the middle of the IMAX shows, but, she's holding her own!

Chapter 17
Higher Education

The bus stopped and lurched as it started up again. It was early morning and it bore few passengers. Opposite Sarah on one of the longitudinal benches sat Lucille, a girl in the next grade. She was a senior, therefore she knew everything.

Lucille was smart and smart-mouthed. There wasn't much news about her that wasn't known by the time the bus reached to high school. Sarah didn't care that much about what Lucille had to say, it was the notebook on her lap that fascinated her. The book was made of some black material. If you had asked Lucille, she would have told you it was leather. Perhaps it was. It was to be used for a class in business, accounting or some such thing. Sarah wanted a book like that. It made Lucille appear older somehow and professional. It was an indicator of station and rank. She was a senior who was soon to graduate and enter the work force.

Going on in school was a struggle for Sarah. Her mother wanted her to leave after high school and get a job to help support her and their household. After all, hadn't Esther and Adam quit school before graduation to help their parents?

Before her Daddy died, he made it clear to her she was not to go beyond high school. "Girls don't go to college" was what he said.

In his family, the oldest brother went to college, then the next oldest. By the time it was his turn his mother was widowed and needed him to help in the family store. Leah, the youngest, a girl, had no chance of reaching her goal of higher education. She took the business curriculum and became a legal secretary. Sarah wondered at this title. Were other secretaries illegal? Sarah's mother, although she did not like Leah, thought being a secretary would be a good profession for Sarah until she met the right man to marry.

Although Sarah had a native talent in the fine arts, she purposely chose science as her field of interest. Biology had appealed to her in her high school classes. It was a way to learn how things worked and to study the mysteries of life which had always fascinated her.

One of her favorite biology teachers was a poet as well. Sarah shared some of her poetry with him. He told her her writing was promising; but as he had done, she must choose a career that would earn her a living wage. Writing poetry might not but teaching would.

So the battle began. She wanted to take academic courses in high school with the goal of becoming a biology teacher. Esther thought that was a colossal waste of time. Hadn't Sarah wasted enough time in high school as it was? How could she waste another four years in college? Was there no end to the demands of this ungrateful child?

Surrounded with piles of her own children's discarded school supplies, Sarah laughed as she recalled the times she pleaded for new notebooks or new pencils. She recalled that day on the bus with Lucille and the beautiful new folder that made her scholarly work legal.

Each year early in September, the ritual of buying school supplies at the corner store began. The teachers would give their lists to the students on the first day of school and by the time Sarah got home and changed her clothes, the line from Lenny's store would extend down the block.

Sarah would read what the teacher wanted to her mother from the list. "Three marble-covered notebooks, a box of sixty-four crayons, a fountain pen", the list went on…

"What do you think, we're made of money? You have some crayons left over from last year when they made you buy such a big box. You didn't even use all the colors!"

"That's what the teacher wants us to get. I can't ignore what she wants."

"I'll have to go speak to the teacher and tell her we can't afford to spend so much on school supplies."

"Please don't do that. I'll try to get by with fewer things."

One happy year, Aunt Leah offered to buy Sarah's school supplies. She took her to Lenny's, Sarah's list in hand. They bought everything on the list including some expensive oilcloth to be used for book covers.

When Esther saw what they had bought she made Leah return a lot of the items but let Sarah keep the oilcloth even though it was a luxury. For many years Sarah used the book covers over again. She kept a piece to cover the pocket French dictionary she used throughout high school and college.

Sarah didn't understand why Esther was so negative about school. Was it because she was left-handed and was told this was a sign of evil when she was switched to the right hand by her teachers? Was she jealous of Sarah's budding theatrical talents and her other gifts in the arts and sciences?

Why did she think Sarah was wasting her time learning the things she loved?

When the time came for a decision about college, Sarah was determined to go and Esther was equally determined for her not to. Sarah had opportunities to attend colleges far from her home on scholarship. This was unthinkable for either of them. How could she leave Esther alone?

A miracle happened. Esther met a man who liked her but did not want to be around Sarah. The feeling was mutual for Sarah who hated him. Even the sound of his voice made her cringe. He was old, he was vile, like the dirty old man in the folk song, "Have Some Madeira".

"Please, God, let him take her away and let me be by myself", she prayed. She had it all planned out. She would go to college and have her own apartment. Esther and Bill would live in luxury in New Jersey where Bill owned a lovely home.

Esther would apologize to Sarah when Bill asked her to go with him on little vacations and not include her. No need. It was a welcome relief to have both of them gone.

Bill told Esther he couldn't be around Sarah because of the emotions she aroused in him. "It's like that movie, 'Lolita'; I can't be around that girl without thinking erotic thoughts about her."

"Ugh. He's perfectly safe with me." Sarah thought.

Unfortunately, Bill's grown children felt negatively about Esther. They saw her as a gold-digger, trying to wrestle their inheritance away from them.

That was the end of the dream. Sarah went to Brooklyn College and lived at home with Esther. It was a reasonable compromise. If Sarah could find a way to go to college for free and provide Esther with continued dependent's benefits, she could live at home and attend college classes.

Years later Sarah found out that Esther had once been a voracious reader. She had read many books that were considered groundbreaking in their time.

When Esther left school to help support her family she went to work in the Theater District in Manhattan. She met many unusual people through her job as a clerk in Walgreen's Pharmacy.

It was the end of the roaring twenties when she began to work. She worked until she married in the late thirties. People from the theater and literary world frequented her store, especially early in the morning after the after-theater parties ended.

Esther became friendly with Eva Le Gallienne, the grand dame of the stage. There was something different about Eva. Esther couldn't quite place what it was. Eva suggested Esther read the new book called "The Well of Loneliness" to better answer her questions.

Transvestites and transsexuals frequented that store, often wearing their stage makeup and costumes.

She came into contact with a young man who was a writer from Great Britain. He had recently moved to New York and was working on several books. She asked him his name and he told her it was difficult for Americans to pronounce but not think "Aldous Huxley" was made up as it really was his name. He ran some of his plots by her, seeing if she liked them and if they should be further developed.

She read a lot of underground material and was quite involved with the artistic counter-culture of the time.

What happened to this curiosity in her?

Was this her act of rebellion against her orthodox upbringing? Was this why, at the age of twenty-seven her family pressured her to marry? She had no desire to marry, to give up her single life, to become like her sisters who wanted only to settle down and raise children.

She would have liked to have a child sometime in her life. She did not want to marry a man in order to have one.

"It's strange now, thinking about this", Sarah mused, "children are now routinely conceived by artificial insemination, many by women who have no interest in marriage or any heterosexual relationship. Gay and lesbian literature have now become classics, required in college classes."

It was akin to watching her own children freely buy the school supplies she used to covet. What she needed then was so out of reach for her. She begged for a chance to go to college. That now is expected as the very least to which her children would aspire.

The structure of the family was changing as well. The traditional two-parent family had found a place among other less traditional configurations; less traditional although no less valuable as forums in which to raise children.

She had heard many people express that the world was changing and not for the better. In her opinion, truth expressed is a healthy thing. Truth repressed may be harmful in ways we cannot imagine.

Chapter 18
All The World's a Stage (Esther's Story)

Finally it is my turn to speak! I have been waiting in the wings so long I thought I'd never be called. I have been a character in so many other stories I wanted to tell my own story in my own way.

I am an actor. That's what I was born to be and that's what I died doing. I played so many roles in my lifetime, I forgot who I was. That is the mark of a great actor, you know, to be able to lose oneself in the role so completely the audience no longer sees an actor on a stage but the character that develops.

I was born in Russia in 1909. My father was in America when I was born so I didn't know him except for photographs and stories I was told about him. My older siblings knew him and used to tease me that I was the only one who had no father at all. They were angry with me that I was born at such an inappropriate time and I was angry with them that they knew my father and I didn't. The mythology around him grew and grew until the time we disembarked at Ellis Island and headed for New York City. He was there to meet us. I was frightened when I saw him for the first time, for to me he was a little picture on a button I wore on my coat. There he was, a giant of a man with a loud voice who embraced my mother and siblings as well as me. We had never met before but they all knew him. We had a lot of catching up to do.

I wanted to be his favorite. I wanted to be like him. I wanted him to love me more than the others. I imitated his every mood and idiosyncrasy. That was the start of my acting career.

The strange this is, the more I acted like him, the more he rejected me! That's a truth that has taken me a long time to understand. We don't like to see ourselves as others see us.

He was a stubborn and severe man as well as one who was sorely misunderstood. He had ideas of how a synagogue should be run, ideas of how it was done in Europe. The American Jews had functioned so long without a European rabbi in many cases they did not want to do things in the European way any longer. It was always a contest of will wherever we went and we moved many times during my childhood.

My mother, siblings and I were seen as a group, "The Rabbi's Wife and Children". We had no identities other than that. Such is the lot of clergy families the world over. We had to behave like "little angels" at all times in public. We weren't. Mama came close most of the time. She was happy to take care of us and of Papa and to fade into the background as people came to tell her how they enjoyed him and his sermons. They asked Mama if she was jealous of all the attention he was getting and she answered with something like "We have nine children, he must pay attention to me at times, too." Somehow this got lost in the translation from the Yiddish when it was retold as it was much funnier in the original. The bottom line is she wished he wouldn't pay so much attention to her, as each pregnancy was a risk to her life.

When they got older they lived apart as she didn't want any more children after Lydia was born when Mama was forty-two. She had her hands full with Lydia from the start and as she was getting older she wanted to do less in taking care of babies, the house and the big, stubborn child who was my Papa.

Why did they have to spoil things by having so many children? As soon as we came to America the babies started coming. I was so jealous of those little ones, the ones born here. There were enough years between us that I had to be their caretaker. My parents told me it was the big sister's job to watch the little ones. I wanted to play like the other children I knew at school. Once, while watching Rachel in her carriage, I dumped her and her carriage into the gutter! Papa was very upset and he punished me severely for it. I told him I didn't mean it but he and I both knew I did, just like when I lied about why I took the eyes out of Fay's doll. He knew I was jealous; but he also knew I was a child and could not understand the seriousness of the things I did.

I was a rebel, that's for sure. I was angry that Sam, the oldest boy got to do things that would get any of us into trouble but he always came out smelling like a rose. He was their favorite. I think the term "favorite son" originated with my parents and Sam.

Girls in those times did not do the things I wanted to do. I wanted to cut my hair and pretend I was a boy and run away from home and join the Army or the circus or anything so I wouldn't have to grow up and get married and have a bunch of children. I was Peter Pan. I was Joan of Arc. I was a girl who didn't want to be one.

I wanted my own space in the house in which to play and dream. Our house was constantly invaded by new babies. Lydia was the last straw! They were so old when she was born they were like grandparents. They were so indulgent they let her get away with everything they were so strict about in the past with the rest of us.

I was a misfit. I did poorly in school because I was left-handed. The teachers switched me to my right hand for writing as I was told left-handed children are evil by nature. I spoke one language at home and another one at school and they switched my writing hand and it was too much for me to handle.

Once I had a teacher who taught us poetry and plays. She had us memorize long passages from Shakespeare and Milton. I loved that! I didn't have to write the words, I had only to memorize them. The teacher spoke in a dramatic way when she recited these works and I learned to imitate her. Shakespeare and Milton spoke so differently from my family. I thought if I were really an American, really educated, I would speak like that, too. When I recited those passages I became my teacher in my voice, my inflection, my mannerisms. The other children laughed at me but I knew I had something they didn't. I had culture.

I wanted to be anyone except who I was; a rabbi's daughter, an immigrant. I wanted to be like everyone else in America, like the people I saw in the movies who were elegant, charming and suave.

When Mama and Papa told me I could quit school at the age of fourteen I jumped at the chance. School was getting incredibly difficult for me. We were starting algebra and science and I wasn't good at those at all. The switching of the hands made everything jumble up in my head and I was finally glad to get away from that confusion.

I got a job in the Theater District in New York City. It was like heaven for me, for here were people acting every day and that was their career. I absorbed the atmosphere and flourished in it.

People there were so different, they made me look like the average American person. Sometimes I even forgot I was a rabbi's daughter. While at work I was just another pretty girl making her way in the world by working as a salesclerk at a pharmacy. I could forget about my non-existent state at home as I interacted with the theater crowd.

I met many celebrities and many who were becoming celebrities. They liked to talk to me about their problems as I was safe and a good listener. To me, their lives were so different I would never expect them to understand any of the rules I had to follow at home. They were Bohemians, they had no rules other than to look beautiful and do the unexpected.

A beautiful young actress who carried an aura of greatness about her came into the store. I wanted to talk to her, to get to know her and find out what it was about her that made her so magnificent. She spoke to me! She became a friend, inviting me to go with her to parties and gallery shoes. I wanted to become like her and asked her about her life and how she started in the theater.

She must have recognized a kindred soul when she looked at me. She told me everything and advised me to read a new book called "The Well of Loneliness" about women like herself and their trials to become recognized as a different type of being, a woman who lived like a man in a man's world.

I was interested. I didn't want to marry a man although my parents saw that as the only option for a young woman. That was our lot in life as dictated by God. "Be fruitful and multiply" was the edict. That's why Mama had so many babies. It was God's will. That's why Papa was angry when she decided to stop having them. She was going against God's will.

Eva Le Gallienne was a woman of a different type. She was an actor of the highest caliber. She performed the classical roles impeccably. All actors admired her skill. I knew her secret. She travelled with a group of people like her; "beautiful misfits", I called them. It was there I felt at home for the first time in my life.

Mama and Papa learned about my dreams to become an actor. This was absolutely forbidden! They were tired of hearing about my lofty aspirations and my desire to leave my mundane existence for the world of the theater.

"I can do this", I told them "a famous actress told me I have talent and the potential to become great, too". All they could think of was what I had told them about Jean Harlow and her mother. "No, no, she's not a movie star like Jean Harlow, she's a classical actress. She calls herself an actor. That's what she is,"

"You will not do this", said Papa," you will not disgrace this family. You know those young men you have been seeing? I want you to choose between the two of them and get married like the rest of your sisters."

I suppose Papa was right.

I was an actress no matter what he said. I could play that role as well as any other.

Chapter 19
Why Have You Forsaken Me?

"I have nothing against her", Freda said " I just don't want you to marry her."

Abe sat and said nothing. He knew enough to always agree with Freda even if he didn't.

Avi, Jacob's brother gloated in triumph. It was through his spying activity that he produced so much negative information about how Sarah would ruin Jacob and his impending career as a physician.

Jacob and Sarah were engaged. After his first year of medical school would be completed and she would graduate from college, they would marry and she would work to support him as he went to school.

Avi had done everything to subvert the engagement and later would do whatever he could to ruin their wedding day. A jealous older brother, he had found a soul-mate in a woman whose younger sister was getting married as well. They became engaged , engaged to be married and in retaliation.

What was the problem with Sarah? She was an orphan and poor, too. She lived with her mother who was a difficult person to get along with. Freda and Abe tried to find something that would estrange her from them.

"She's not Jewish, she's Chinese!"

"She's as Jewish as you are, Ma. Her grandfather was a rabbi."

"Whatever she is, she is not like us. She's an orphan."

Sarah wondered if losing her father wasn't punishment enough. These people acted as if she had murdered him.

She could not understand what she had done to alienate them other than to love her son.

That son was the one they never expected to amount to much. Now, he was on his way to becoming a doctor. That was a surprise! Avi, the genius, was the one with all the talent and brains in the family as if these things were given out in restricted amounts. Jacob was not as bright but he was an overachiever who had a goal. He was going to go to medical school. His school was in Pittsburgh, far away from them and from Sarah as well. "That's not such a bad thing; maybe he will meet someone more suitable for him and forget about Sarah. He was young, only twenty-one years old." thought Freda.

They threatened to disown him if he and Sarah married and they did.

Why did Sarah continue with this relationship? Hadn't she had enough hardship? Why complicate her life by marrying into a family that didn't want her?

What the family did not know was that Sarah had had a dream

One night after a particularly bad time with her prospective in-laws she was ready to call off the engagement and let them live out their lives in peace and contentment.

She dreamt about a vast field of wheat. The wheat was golden, gently blowing in the wind. The field extended far beyond what the eye could see. She was walking in this field with Jacob. They held hands and spoke softly to each other.

She heard music in the air. It was an old song she loved. The tune was "Eli, Eli", a song from the Yiddish Theater. She liked to hear her father play it on the piano while Aunt Pauline sang.

It was a song about the trials Jewish people have had over time. The first line is from Psalm 22, "Eli, Eli, why have you forsaken me?"

Although the song tells of trials it says that through the Lord and only through the Lord are we to be saved.

The music in the dream was that of the old song but the language wasn't Yiddish. The language of the song was unknown to her. It wasn't Hebrew either although it sounded a bit like Hebrew. It was a tongue she had never heard before yet it seemed vaguely familiar as if she knew what it was telling her.

A voice in the dream told her that she and Jacob would marry as that had been predetermined. She would have many trials and she would know how to handle them. Their love and their future life were more important than any petty problem they had at any time. They would have many children and their offspring would be as wheat in the field, just as the offspring of Abraham and Sarah were as numerous as the stars in the sky.

Whatever doubts Sarah had about the forthcoming wedding were removed by the message of that dream.

Chapter 20
Patterns

When Esther went on a visit to her doctor it was often associated with a side trip to visit her sister, Rachel who lived across the street from Dr. Simeone's office on Ocean Avenue.

Dr. Simeone's office was in a building made of orange bricks. Rachel's was on the same side of the street across Beverly Road. Beverly Road was the street Sarah saw from the windows of her apartment. It extended from her neighborhood, Kensington, to Flatbush Avenue which was well over a mile to the north. Ocean Avenue was a large street parallel to Flatbush. One could see the stores on Flatbush Avenue as one stood in front of Dr. Simeone's building.

The doctor visits and the visits to Rachel's were often concluded with shopping trips. From Beverly and Flatbush they walked to Church and Flatbush. These streets started out one block apart as they intersected Ocean Parkway. They spread out as legs of a triangle that became almost ten blocks apart on Flatbush Avenue. The entire span of Flatbush Avenue between Church and Beverly was lined with stores on both sides of the street. What fun it was to go shopping on those days!

The doctor's office was decorated in the austere style one would expect from a bachelor whose specialty was the female reproductive system. Oriental rugs covered dark wooden floors. Dark and dull art prints graced the walls. This was definitely a place for adults only. Often, nuns were seated in the waiting room when Sarah and Esther entered.

Dr. Simeone was a Roman Catholic and had an excellent reputation as a physician. The nuns of his church trusted him and were his patients, too.

Sarah was curious about the nuns. They appeared to her to be angels dressed in white habits. They had a quality of serenity about them which she had not seen in other people. If there were angels in this doctor's waiting room, surely he was ordained by God to heal people.

"Who are they?" Sarah asked her mother when she was four years old.

Her mother began to explain as one of the nuns went on to say that they taught children in school. They said when Sarah would be old enough to go to school they would be her teachers.

Sarah was anxious to go to school to see those angels again. Her mother told her they taught in a special school where people who belonged to a different religion went to school. Sarah's teachers would not be dressed in white habits like the women in the doctor's office.

Years later, Esther would tell Sarah that before she had married Sarah's father she had dated Dr. Simeone. When they seriously considered marriage, Esther asked her father what he would think if she married outside her faith.

"It is not allowed", he replied "although he is a fine man and a respected physician, he is not Jewish."

Case closed.

When Sarah and Jacob were engaged they were separated for a year while Jacob attended medical school in Pittsburgh and Sarah completed her college degree in Brooklyn.

Sarah's favorite aunt, Leah, had taken pity on the poor love-sick Sarah and offered to pay for her to take a trip to visit Jacob. How was she to get there? The only way to make the trip in a short enough time was to fly both ways.

Sarah had always been afraid of heights. Her father's death on the Brooklyn Bridge didn't lessen that fear.It multiplied it by powers of ten. How would she be able to do this? In this case, love was stronger than fear and she made plans for the plane trip.

It was a time when students could get seats on airlines for a low cost by flying "standby". It was quite a bargain and made Leah's gift go even farther. Sarah was alone as she waited for her plane, the plane that would take her to Pittsburgh and to Jacob. In the waiting area, also waiting to board was a nun, dressed in her full white habit. The Sister was probably as nervous about flying as Sarah as she sat, busily praying her rosary.

Sarah was relieved to know if one of those angels was with them on the plane, everything would be fine, no matter what happened.

After the takeoff and a slight feeling of disorientation as the plane made a steep turn, Sarah courageously looked out her window. There below her was New Jersey. She recognized it from the map! She saw rivers and lakes and the "What was that?" It looked like a deep green carpet draped over the hills. She looked over at the Sister who smiled back at her.

Then Sarah had her epiphany. That was the word for it, she was certain. She had encountered that word for the first time in James Joyce's "Portrait of The Artist as a Young Man". Epiphany. The green carpet over the hills was made of trees. At this altitude, the trees made a velvety cover for the hills. In the same way individual fibers of a carpet stand next to each other on a carpeted floor; in the same way ribosomes on the endoplasmic reticulum stand together in the electron microscope photographs Sarah had recently seen in the laboratory.

Sarah had always known there was a creative force in the universe. She had not realized before how the Creator used patterns that repeated in order to form what was created. Now, distanced from the creation she lived in, she saw it all with new eyes.

"It's all the same", she thought "from the largest to the smallest. We are all made of the same stuff in the same way." She had an idea about that when she studied comparative anatomy but did not fully understand until she saw the figures of the animals from the air. The big mammals on the farms below were the same shape as the little mammals she worked with in the laboratory. The trees and the broccoli she ate for dinner and the organelles in the cell had the same basic pattern. She developed this concept in her mind calling the organic material "God's Play-Dough". This organic material could be morphed into various forms of various sizes but certain patterns governed the direction of their growth and development. All that information was coded in the genetic material and was the pattern to make "God's Play-Dough" into different forms for different functions.

She knew that whatever would happen to her, she was made of the same stuff that would eventually be recycled in the created universe and also that she was an observer, watching and learning to untangle the mysteries of that universe. The part of her that was doing the watching was not a part of that. It was not made of "God's Play-Dough". The part of her that was doing the watching was not made of anything. It was watching through her eyes but her eyes weren't her. The thing she called "herself" was eternal and had existed for all time and would continue to exist beyond her physical death.

Chapter 21
Genevieve Has The Key

They were six girls living in apartment houses numbered 250 and 240 Ocean Parkway. They were inseperable, all about the same age, playing together on the sidewalks and each other's homes.

They attended different school, some the public school and others the Immaculate Heart of Mary Catholic School (or IHM as it was affectionately known).

The girls who went to the public schools were envious of those who went to IHM as they were given so many holidays. Often, when the public school group were on their way home from school, the IHM girls were outside playing in the street. They had been home all day celebrating some exotic saint's day or day of obligation by playing outside.

Sarah was confused by this as when she had a religious holiday it was spent wearing uncomfortable dress clothes which were not to get soiled and play was absolutely forbidden as it was offensive to God.

It all evened out as the nuns at IHM were strict in their discipline and knuckles were often hit with rulers and penances were given out freely for minor rule infractions.

In the summertime when there was no school, all the girls played outside and in the lobbies of their buildings if it was raining. What did they play? "School", of course.

Genevieve and Sarah shared a secret. The mailboxes for their apartment house were organized in two areas of the lobby. The apartments whose letters began with the beginning of the alphabet were on the north side of the building. The later letters' mailboxes were on the south side. They would often stand and watch the mail carrier sort the mail into the various boxes through a large opening above the bank of boxes. They would open their families' respective boxes and bring the mail to their apartments. On one occasion, Genevieve had forgotten her mail key. "Here, try mine." Sarah said. It fit!

"Don't tell anyone about this, it's our secret. We must promise not to let anyone know these keys are the same or they will make us change them; but if one of us forgets her key, we will always have a spare."

Another secret of Genevieve was that although her mother was a Roman Catholic, her father was Jewish. He didn't attend church with his wife and children and no one saw him at synagogue either. His faith was known to him alone although his children were raised in the Catholic faith and attended IHM.

It was not unusual in the early fifties to encounter people with few relatives, especially those of Jewish heritage as families were thinned out in Europe during the Holocaust. No one mentioned the absence of relatives on Genevieve's fathers' side. Her mother had plenty of family so Genevieve has many aunts, uncles and cousins.

The girls grew older and went to high school. The Catholic girls stayed at IHM and the others went to Erasmus Hall. This time of life was busy for the girls as they made new friends and moved their plans along toward the future. It was a shock when they learned Genevieve was going to join a convent and become a nun!

What would be the most awful thing a young girl would chose to do in the early sixties? Become a nun, for sure. That had to be the worst choice anyone could ever make according to the other friends. Poor Genevieve! While she looked forward to her sacred marriage, the other girls acted as if she were going to her own funeral while still alive.

Sarah and the others went on to college and careers and marriages while Genevieve disappeared. Nuns weren't allowed many family visits during the pre-Vatican II days. Who knew where she was?

When Sarah started medical school she became friendly with a nun of an order similar to Genevieve's. Sister Elizabeth was a great source of information about the things Sarah wanted to know. She imagined her friend Genevieve went through similar experiences as Elizabeth did before Vatican II. Afterwards thing changed radically in the orders. The nuns were allowed to wear ordinary clothing and habits became optional. They even wore a little makeup and Elizabeth had pierced ears! Elizabeth was studying medicine after having been a high school teacher for many years.

Sarah and Elizabeth hung out together in medical school. Sarah was one of the few who was married and had a child. She did not participate in the social scene of medical students nor did Elizabeth. They became good friends.

When Sarah finished medical school, she and Elizabeth parted company for residencies in different places. Sarah went into surgery and Elizabeth into family practice at opposite ends of the state of Pennsylvania.

Sarah had many mentors in her medical studies, many of them women. Dr. Sembrot was a woman surgeon who was married to a minister. What a strange combination! Although Ellen Sembrot was a Christian believer and a minister's wife, she was not a proselytizer and did not talk about her faith in medical circles. She demonstrated her faith in the way she treated others. She was a loving person.

Sarah knew this woman was special and different from other teachers she had had. Was she simply a kind person or was there something else, some other quality Sarah had missed?

Surgical residency was difficult. It required long hours of work in the operating room, the emergency room, the intensive care unit and the follow-up clinic. In addition to that, Sarah had family responsibilities; two small children and her aging mother to care for. Her mother had helped her care for her children since their births and it was now that Sarah had increased concerns, fearing the worst whenever Esther took them outside of the house, as Esther's eyesight and hearing were deteriorating rapidly. Her mother was so fond of the children. Sarah felt it was impossible to ask her to participate any less in their care although it was a cause for constant surveillance.

Throughout this period, Ellen was a strong support. She was an example of a woman who had been through this training period herself under similar conditions. When she had told her own husband she was tired. Exhausted in fact, after a particularly grueling weekend on-call, he told her not to complain, that it was her choice to become a surgeon. She never complained again.

Ellen was the light at the end of her tunnel. Sarah sighed, expressing her wish for a "normal" life once again. "If only I could sit down for a few hours and read a novel just for pleasure. I feel like I have lost my life, the life in which I was a human being."

Ellen assured her that the time would come when it would be possible to once again enjoy those simple human pleasures so many take for granted.

It was toward the end of Sarah's residency that she began to have recurrent dreams. In her dream she was living once again in the apartment house on Ocean Parkway. She hadn't been there for years, why was she back again? She would go to the mailbox. Her mailbox was stuffed with mail from all the years she had been gone. She couldn't get all the mail out no matter how hard she tried.

Night after night she had the same dream and woke with frustration. "What is the message about the mail and the mailbox?"

It was at the same time she began to have her spiritual crisis. She felt as if the Hound of Heaven was biting constantly at her heels. It would not stop until she did something. What was it she was to do?

She thought of Ellen. What was it that made her different from her other teachers? It was not that she was a woman and a parent, too. It was that she was a Christian. Sarah knew that in addition to helping her with her residency and life questions, Ellen was praying for her. Could it be that Ellen cared enough to want to pray for her? This was something new for Sarah. Prayers in her life had been to God to help care for the sick and infirm. She wasn't sick or infirm, simply tired. No, she was sick! She was spiritually sick. Her spirit was dying as she went through the motions of living.

Her mailbox was stuffed with old mail that had accumulated over the years since she was a child, one of six girls who lived and played together. One of them had become a nun and had given her life to Christ.

Genevieve had the key.

Chapter 22
A Leap of Faith

Jacob and Sarah had been married for almost ten years. Both were busy with their careers as well as raising two children. Sarah's mother was living with them, helping out with the children while they endured the rigors of medical training and practice in a large eastern city.

One day, as Sarah was getting ready to leave for the hospital, she heard a voice whisper in her ear. She recognized that voice immediately as that of "The Narrator", the one who helped her in her early life by explaining her dreams. The Narrator said, "You will join a church." It seemed like a good idea. Her children were getting older, the boy in the first grade and the girl in Montessori pre-school. Religious education was something Sarah wanted for her children.

"Times have changed," she thought, "when I was a girl, girls didn't go to Hebrew School. Now it is the current thing to do to have a Bat Mitzvah. Joining a synagogue would be a good thing. Little Adam will have to be Bar Mitzvah and six is not too early to start his Hebrew education."

Inquiries were made about which synagogue to join. They decided upon one that was near their home where many of their colleagues also worshipped. They went through the process of joining and getting Adam enrolled in Hebrew School. Sarah was happy to be providing her children with something her parents didn't give her. She was also feeling a sense of finally belonging in a community.

The voice kept telling her the same thing, "You will join a church."

"I did that", she said ", we belong to the Reform Temple. Our son is enrolled in religious school."

The Narrator's voice would not go away. It was insistent.

"Sorry, wrong number", she thought. "We are Jewish, we belong to a synagogue. That's our church."

Some things happened at the temple which made Sarah concerned. Some things were done she felt were not particularly caring. She grinned and bore it for she felt the need for religious education for her children overcame the petty social slights. After all, these things happen in every community group, they are not unique to religious institutions.

Little Adam came home from Sunday school one day announcing, "I'm so glad we are Jewish!"

"Why is that?" Sarah asked.

"Because we are better than other people."

She began to understand slowly why the voice of the narrator kept insisting they change their church affiliation.

"Something is wrong here," she said to Jacob, "I don't want my child to learn things like that. It is not consistent with my understanding of what the Bible has to say about being a good Jew."

It was indeed a rare occasion when the whole family was able to take a trip into the city. Everyone's schedules were so rigid and demanding that a weekend day-off for both parents was a rarity. They planned to go to the Art Museum on a Saturday afternoon. The museum was one of Sarah's favorite places. She went to the exhibit of medieval art. She loved the ancient tapestries, especially the one of the Lady and the Unicorn. On the way to that exhibit, a large wooden crucifix from that period hung in an archway. The Christ figure was depicted in such a way that the horrors of the crucifixion were graphic and evident. She stared at the figure, transfixed, as if she had never before seen it in exactly that way. "Why are you persecuting me?" The figure seemed to speak to her.

The image of the crucified Christ stayed in Sarah's mind throughout the day. She had not yet read the New Testament. It was a book that was forbidden to her. In the Jewish faith, the Bible ends with the end of the Old Testament. Anything added to that was a sacrilege, a heresy. She decided to take a leap of faith and read the New Testament even though this act was risky. She had been told it was full of blasphemy and lies. She thought of the stories she had heard of her Grandfather Mordechai and his encounter with the Christian church in Russia. He was one of the learned men of his generation. He had even studied Kabbalah! She knew she wasn't old enough to study Kabbalah. Perhaps the New Testament would illuminate some thoughts from the master teacher, Jesus, and help calm her religious unrest by putting the issue of Christianity and the New Testament to rest forever.

She read the New Testament in its entirety in one sitting. How much easier it was to read than the Old. By the time she had finished, she realized Jesus was the one He said He was. He was the Messiah promised to deliver Israel. She wanted to become a Christian, to follow this teacher, this Son of God, as his was the right way. She was sorry for the

129

persecution of that early Christian church from the time of its inception by Saul and others. If God could call Saint Paul, a.k.a. Saul, to become a Christian, He could call any Jewish person.

There remained the problem of what to do about the Sunday school. Jacob and Sarah discussed it. "You can do whatever you want about the temple", Sarah said, " I am not interested in going back there. If you want to send Adam to another school, that's fine. I am not happy keeping him in that one."

"What are we going to do?" said Jacob.

"Do what you want. I'm not going back to that temple or any other one."

"Don't you want him to be Bar Mitzvah?"

"If he wants to, that's fine. I am not going back to temple."

"What are you saying?"

"I don't know. I'm thinking about something else."

The voice kept plaguing her," You will join a church!"

"Which one?"

"What about the one where your children go to school?"

That was a real puzzler. That was spoken in the way of an Old Testament prophet. She had just planned to take a child out of a religious school because she was told to join a church and now she was to put him back in and rejoin that temple.

She thought for a while about this enigma and then realized that the building the Montessori school her children attended was on the property of a church. The Montessori building was owned by the Episcopal Church.

She arranged a meeting with the priest of that church to ask him some questions.

In the interim, Jacob thinking his wife had lost her mind chose to read the New Testament to see what had caused this complete turnabout. He was beginning to warm up to the idea of conversion himself although nowhere near convinced it was the right thing to do. He agreed to go with Sarah to meet with the priest if only to ask some questions, too.

No one was more astonished than the Episcopal priest when he received the phone call telling him a Jewish couple was interested in exploring the Christian faith.

Sarah sat in Father Sam's office thinking how dreary and dull it must be to be a minister in the Episcopal Church.

Father Sam sat looking at this couple, thinking "Woody Allen and Barbra Streisand were now sitting opposite him to tell him they want to become Christians."

Everything in the office was decorated with crosses. Everything was black including all the vestments Father Sam wore except for his collar.

In spite of the culture shock, they got along well. Father Sam answered their questions. They asked for some reading material to better understand the faith.

"That's what everyone asks", Father Sam thought, "they're not so different from Christian people after all."

"He seems like a nice enough guy, he has a sense of humor." They thought.

Father Sam had a new associate, a woman who was recently ordained to the priesthood. At this time, it was revolutionary as women had just received permission to become priests in the Episcopal Church, perhaps a year before. "Mother Judith" was a very young woman with bright red hair. She was fresh out of seminary. Sarah and Jacob became her project.

Often they would simply stare at each other.

Judith was uneasy. She felt the need to apologize for the Holocaust. In her mind, all Christians were guilty of the travesty that was delivered to the Jews in Eastern Europe. Sarah and Jacob assured her they had wrestled with that many times. They believed the people responsible for that horror did not represent the teachings of Jesus in the world. Although they were Christians in name, they were not Christians in their actions.

"Why had they come to the church? What was the impetus?" Judith asked.

"You'd never believe me if I told you how it happened", Sarah thought.

"We really don't understand it ourselves", they answered "but we are here now and we want to be baptized into the Christian faith. Not only we, but our children and Sarah's mother would like to join the church.

Father Sam picked up his phone and called the Bishop.

"You'll never believe this." he said "An entire family of Jewish people wants to join our church!"

Chapter 23
The New Year

Once again it was time for the High Holy Days. Each year was bittersweet at this time; this was the time for endings and beginnings. The season of growth was over and the harvest began. The leaves turned and the light changed. It was fall.

Daddy had been gone for twenty years! Still, at this time of year, his memory was renewed as if his death had just occurred. This year was different from the rest as Sarah had decided to become a Christian.

"What will happen to me?" she thought as she considered her Jewish roots. This was the time of year when God reviewed your deeds of the previous year and decided if you would be inscribed in the Book of Life for another year. If you atoned properly for your sins, another year was added.

A Jew is placed on earth to serve God in the way God has intended for him to serve. You must not try to be something you are not.

Sarah wrestled with this thought.

"If He didn't want me to be a Christian, why did He ask me to join a church? Why did he send his son, Jesus, to redeem first the Jews and then the Gentiles? Does this redemption override the need to atone on Yom Kippur in order to be inscribed in the Book of Life?

Jesus instituted the Eucharist at a Passover seder. He used elements of that well-known ritual to create a new one so we would always remember Him. It was like remembering Daddy at the time of the High Holy Days. The memory was always there, but at that time of year, the presence of the memory was amplified as if he were really walking with me. Isn't that our Yom Kippur? Isn't this how we atone for our sins at confession at the Lord's Supper? What about the Book of Life? 'I am the resurrection and the life, he that believes in me shall not die but have eternal life.' That's what He said. I'll take my chances."

That year instead of going to the synagogue, Sarah and her family went to church to worship at the time of the High Holy Days. Although they felt somewhat uneasy at first, watching to people go up to the altar for communion relieved their fears. They could not yet participate as they had not yet been baptized. That would happen later, in October.

The altar was the great equalizer. Every person who was baptized and believed Jesus was the Messiah could come to the altar and receive His body and blood. With the exception of the smallest children, everyone who was baptized could receive at their church.

Witnessing this first mass, Sarah sat in awe of the profundity of this simple act. Not only was the liturgy beautifully sung and spoken, the music of the setting of the mass was uplifting even if its harmonies were unfamiliar. Sarah had always associated prayer with melodies heard in the synagogue, melodies in a minor key. "This will take a little getting used to", she thought as she listened to the Healy Willan setting.

She was instructed that although she could not yet receive communion, she was welcome to come to the altar to receive a blessing. She had given her life to Christ. Waiting for baptism was waiting for the time this would become public knowledge. She would wait and watch patiently.

It was as it was written in the New Testament. The priest offered the body and blood to the kneeling worshippers. How simple it was and yet how moving. The elements, the bread and the wine had become the body and blood of Christ. As a scientist, Sarah knew they were bread and wine. As a believer, she knew they were flesh and blood.

"This will be a stumbling block to the learned" she thought. How true.

"I didn't see you at the temple" her friends remarked after Rosh Hashonah.

" I have become a Christian. I was at church."

"No matter what you do, you'll always be a Jew"

How could she explain what she did not understand either? Was being a Jew a religious designation or something else?

Of course, she would always be a Jew. All her ancestors were Jewish from the beginning of time. As far as she knew, this pedigree remained unbroken from biblical time. As far as she knew, that is. No one had ever contested it. Who knew how they had gotten to Eastern Europe in the first place? All she knew was that there were many dispersions of Jews over the course of written history and her ancestors lived in Russia in the nineteenth century. Before that, who knows? The records were not available to her as they were destroyed either in the Pogroms or in World War II.

What was she, then? The best description she could think of was a "Jewish Christian" like those described in the Epistles. Like Saint Paul, her role model.

Saint Paul was a persecutor of the early church, a Jew who lived in Tarsus: A Jew who spoke Greek and read Hebrew, a man of the dispersion. He was a Roman citizen by default. What was his identity? What was hers?

She had lived all her life as a Jew, yet by birth she was an American. As all first-generation Americans, there was a place her family had lived before. Was she Russian? A Russian-American? A Russian-American Jewish-Christian female surgeon mother wife daughter?

Did any other ethnic group have a similar problem? Did the Irish, Italians or Germans? When they immigrated to America they were identified by their country of origin, not by their religious beliefs. Did everyone assume a French person was a Roman Catholic because that is the dominant religion in that country? What about the Huguenots? Why then did being a Russian-Jewish ancestry automatically make one a practicing Jew?

She supposed it was a result of the Jews continually living as a religious minority within the countries of their dispersion and being given the directive not to assimilate within the larger culture by their religious leaders. Not assimilating was the most important thing. If a Jew were to think of marrying a member of the larger (non-Jewish) culture, that person would have to convert to Judaism before the marriage could take place. The purpose was to keep the Jewish culture alive.

Sarah had performed an act that removed her from that culture and placed her within the larger culture of Christians of all nationalities.

When Saint Paul became an apostle, he was sent out to preach the good news to the people he had been actively persecuting. They often doubted his sincerity, thinking he was perpetrating some plot to destroy them. He was often viewed as a "mole", operating within enemy lines.

How could they not feel that way based on his prior acts? He spent the rest of his life preaching the good news to the Gentiles. Paul was a different person than he was before his encounter with the Lord on the road to Damascus. It took a little work to convince the followers of The Way that he was no longer their enemy, that he was one of their own.

Was he still Jewish? Yes. Did he deny that? No. What he did say was that it was no longer important. It wasn't necessary to become a Jew to become a Christian. The Way was open to Jew or Greek, slave or free, male or female. Once a person put on the garment of Christ he became a new creation. He became an adopted child of the Father.

It was amusing that she had to be re-adopted into a religion that originated with the faith of her ancestors.

Sarah had read the New Testament as she had read the Old Testament and believed it as it was written at the historic time it was written. She wasn't thinking about the centuries of culture that had come between the writing of it and her reading it.

How simple it would be if the words were read without debate about their literal meaning and application for the current culture.

The Old Testament prophets predicted the appearance of the Messiah. The Jews still await his coming, not having accepted Jesus as the promised anointed one.

The Jewish Christians at the time of Paul accepted the divinity of Jesus and spread that news to the civilized world as they knew it.

It must have been difficult to make that determination two thousand years before as there were many claiming to be the Messiah at that time. Sarah had the advantage of the test of time. She knew her choice was the correct one based upon scripture. She believed that as a Jew and a Christian.

Chapter 24
In Limbo

Once again she found herself in that world lit a twilight were nothing happened. Nothing ever happened here. There was no motion. The streets were empty, void of people as she made her way along Ocean Parkway on her way home. She walked as one walking through sand.

"I have to cross the street," she thought "but I can't move fast enough to get across before the light will change." She rose up, flying above the street, above the benches and the roof tops. The street lights were on but they didn't illuminate this world of perpetual dusk.

Sarah knew as she began to fly this was a dream. She had had lucid dreams for as long as she could remember. Flying was one signal the dream was lucid. Now that she was aware she was dreaming she could manipulate the dream on her own.

Who was she looking for? She was looking for her father. He was here someplace. Why couldn't she find him? Everything was frozen in time. It was the day he died.

Over and over she would have this dream. This one made her restless as if she needed to do something but did not know how to act. It made her feel as if she were truly alone, searching for something in a world of no motion, a world of little light. As years went by, finding her father in this dream seemed more fruitless.

About two years after she had begun to explore the Christian faith, after she had become a member of a church, she had a vision.

Her vision was not a dream, not in her usual way of dreaming. She was fully conscious of things happening around her as she sat in meditation. Her husband came into the room as did her children and they spoke to her as she witnessed this waking vision.

She had been preparing a forum on Christian meditation and had asked her spiritual director for some help. Anne, the rector's wife was her spiritual director. She had suggested a scene to use in meditation.

"Imagine you are floating in the water on the Sea of Galilee…"

She looked at the shore and saw Jesus standing there.

He was enveloped in a whirling, spiral cloud of light. All around the cloud were sparkling objects that shone like thousands of eyes. The cloud was so bright and fear provoking she could not look at it without experiencing physical pain.

"Is that you, Lord?" she asked "I want to see you but I can't bear your appearance. Human eyes are not used to so much motion and light."

"Forgive me, I forgot." He said and appeared in a way she might look at him although his eyes continued to emit two clear and piercing beams of blue light.

He opened his arms and drew her toward him. She was drawn into the center of his body, into his heart.

He asked, "Is there something I can do to help you?"

In his heart was total peace and stillness. She could rest there forever and experience this blissful feeling of pure love.

She thought about the souls of her father and Grandma Rivka both of whom had died without knowing Christ.

Sarah told Jesus about this and he told her to pray for them.

He took her to her church and she sat in her usual pew. A mass was about to begin although Sarah was the only worshipper.

She knelt down and prayed for the souls of her departed father and grandmother.

Up above her on the Rood Screen was Jesus, crucified. He was dying in agony. Tears came to her eyes. Tears came to Jesus' eyes on the cross as well.

The priest blessed the sacraments of bread and wine. When he broke the communion wafer she heard Jesus say, "I died to save ALL of you."

She received the sacraments and found herself in her childhood home with Jesus at her side.

She asked Him where the soul of her father was. Jesus indicated it was exactly where it was when she "left" him. It was in that twilight world she called limbo.

The day of her father's death was then recreated completely to the smallest detail. She was sitting beside him on the convertible sofa watching television. She and her father were in pajamas, he in his favorite striped ones. He was unshaven. She looked at her father's face which she barely remembered and he was just as he was on that day.

Her father must have seen Jesus standing near them for he knelt and bent his head as if in prayer. Jesus said to Sarah, "Do what you must do."

She looked at him in puzzlement and then she knew exactly what she was to do. She cupped her hands and held them over her father's bald head. She said, "Adam Gilbert, I baptize you in the name of the Father and of the Son and of the Holy Spirit, as it was in the beginning, is now and ever shall be, world without end, amen."

Torrents of water poured from her hands and she knew this came from God himself. She looked at Jesus as if to tell him the power of the water was overwhelming, that again, she was only human and not used to God's force. The waterfall stopped.

"Go on." Jesus said, "Do the rest." The rest?

She thought for a while and proceeded to make the sign of the cross with her finger on his forehead and say, "Now you are Christ's own forever."

Her grandmother came in from the bedroom she and Sarah shared. Sarah did the same for her.

Sarah returned with Jesus to the Sea of Galilee. She looked at the clear sky and saw a tiny figure suspended far above in the air. She watched as Jesus ascended toward that figure. "It must be Mary." she thought as she watched his form grow smaller.

That was the end of the waking vision.

Sarah knew something extraordinary had taken place even if this was not consistent with the teachings of her church.

"He died to save ALL of us." She pondered this over and over again. "That is what he said; even those in that twilight world."

Limbo! That's where she went in dreams night after night looking for her father. That was the place of no motion, the dim world.

She pondered the words Jesus said, "Where you left him." She hadn't thought she had left her father. He had left her when he died.

She had the dream one final time. A huge shaft of light illuminated the dreamscape, breaking into the twilight and dispersing it. She felt as if a great burden was lifted from her and if she never accomplished anything more in her life, she had done what was necessary to do.

Chapter 25
How Should I Know?

Violet and Sarah sat on matching reclining chairs in Violet's living room. They had enjoyed a light lunch and now were talking as if they had been friends for years.

Violet was Sarah's spiritual advisor, her new spiritual advisor assigned to her since she told Father Sam about her vision. She was reassigned for Anne didn't know what to do with someone who had had a vision.

"I'm here because they say I am a mystic and that you are one, too. What is a mystic?"

"How in hell should I know?"

They laughed.

Violet was an older woman who had come late in life to the priesthood. She was almost as old as Sarah's parents although she had the untiring energy of a much younger woman. After a short conversation Sarah learned that Violet had lived most of her life in a neighborhood in Brooklyn near where Sarah had grown up.

Violet's house was an enchanting place. A trellis in the yard held grapes which were in blossom. Tom, Violet's husband loved birds and had built an aviary which spanned three floors of their house.

Books were found in every room of the house on every available shelf and surface. There were books about religion, spirituality, history; all were welcome and well read. Violet had read a lot and lived a long time. She knew well how to comfort a person whose life was falling apart as hers had done so on many occasions.

They didn't talk about Violet's struggles. They talked about Sarah's; but unlike Anne who had told Sarah to put them behind her and get on with her life, Violet helped her understand why that was the most difficult thing to do.

They met often after that first meeting, usually once a week. More than talking or meditating (as mystics are known to do), Sarah learned a way of life. There was a way to honor God's purpose in one's life and always be open to hear His voice when He called. There was a way to be kind and thoughtful without asking for anything in return. There was a way to look at one's oppressors with love and caring and to be able to say, "Forgive them for they know not what they do."

Often they talked about books and Sarah benefitted from Violet's rich store of them. The greatest gift Violet gave her was the gift of time. When can one find time to pray and meditate in a day of constant activity? "When you are alone in your car you can meditate. You have those times in the day when you are driving back and forth from the hospital."

Sarah learned that a contemplative life may be lived in the midst of chaos; that one can be in the world and not of it. She suspected she could do this as earlier in her life when she first opened her eyes on planet Earth it was her natural state.

The world she entered when she went to sleep was the world of the spirit, the world that was real to her. She was instructed by an unseen narrator when she was very young and could not make sense of that world or of the physical world of time and space. As she grew older, she began to understand the rules of both worlds and how to keep them separate. The voice became less necessary, only offering explanations when she specifically asked for help.

"But he never left. He was there to whisper in my ear 'You will join a church'," she thought.

In her dream world time was absent. The living and the dead mingled in a concert out of sequence in time. She learned the shorthand of her personal dream language, her doorway into the archetypal language of ancient thought and religious faith.

She set up her own system for the categorizing of her dreams. Often, this was at odds with the classical Freudian psychology of dreams she had learned in medical school although not at all unfamiliar to the Jungians.

She began to keep a record of her dreams and look for meaning in their messages. Most of her dreams were mundane, concerned with events and problems of daily life. Even those considered lucid were primarily of use for problem solving in the world of time and space.

Occasionally her dreams became more vivid and symbolic. These were the ones she considered "religious" in nature. They offered answers to questions of the nature of human existence. It was these she linked with the concept of the "collective unconscious".

Other dreams were for her guidance. They were rare and helped her make decisions like when to marry and whom. They contained information about her future, about the births of her own children and their names. She looked upon these as messages from God, like those mentioned in the Bible given to Jacob and Joseph.

Waking visions were different. These were more real than "reality" or the most vivid of her dreams. They were visions given directly from God while she was awake and aware of being within time and outside of time at once. This was the vision of Jesus baptizing her deceased father and grandmother.

The vision and the telling of it was a turning point. Telling it opened "Pandora's box" in the church she attended. She learned after she told it to father Sam and his wife Anne (her former spiritual advisor) she would not tell it again to anyone who would not understand its origin and purpose.

It was the most important thing in Sarah's life. To know that her beloved father and grandmother were safe with the Lord Jesus and that she had been a witness to that and a part of that action was so gratifying to know that if she never accomplished anything else in her lifetime, her life's purpose was fulfilled.

The responses she received from that little audience surprised her. The first from Anne "I've been meditating for years and have not had even one little experience of the numinous. I'm very jealous."

From Father Sam "I know this is important to you but there can be an outpouring of images associated with certain emotional states that would encourage the imagination to… blah, blah, blah."

She learned to keep it to herself as she kept other visions. Not consciously wanted to do anything wrong she found herself invoking heresies unknown to her.

Is there any reason to find this sort of activity of Spirit unusual in a religion that is based upon the visions of biblical figures for the past few thousand years?

Sarah was not the first or last person to have this type of vision. She was not the only "mystic whatever the hell that is."

"Look at Saint Paul," she thought, "what could be more unbelievable than his experience on the road to Damascus? Is there any reason to believe God has stopped interacting with his created beings or that what He reveals to them is not the truth?"

Chapter 26
Don't Tell Anyone

In the story of the raising of Jairus' daughter from the dead in the Gospel of Luke, Jairus is admonished not to tell anyone what happened.

Why, if one's daughter had died and was resurrected to health would one not want to tell anyone what happened?

Sarah pondered over this as she pondered over many things she encountered in both the Old and New Testaments.

After she had lived as a Christian for more than twenty years, she began to understand why Jesus had counseled Jairus in this way.

The Kingdom of God is unlike a kingdom in the world. God is a better parent than any human would ever be or aspire to become. God loves all of us, unconditionally. When one becomes a Christian, ideally, one recognizes God's love and the kingdom is present within each of us.

Not so of us humans who are a little more narrow-minded.

Jesus said people would leave father and mother to follow him and that belief in him would split families apart. Such was the case with Sarah and her family.

Her in-laws, who were never fond of her, found new reasons to dislike her. It was fortunate the conversion happened after her mother-in-law had passed away. Who could imagine the scale of disruption of the family if she were still alive then it occurred? Freda was the matriarch, the prime mover of the family and the glue that held them together. This act would cause a war!

Her father-in-law whose own brother changed his name to appear "less Jewish" thought he understood. "You did it for business reasons, right?"

He was told it was done for reasons of faith. Business had nothing to do with it. "So, what do you do as a Christian? Do you go to church?"

The lack of understanding of this man boggled Sarah's mind along with his ethics. He never met the two younger children of Sarah and Jacob born after the conversion.

"Why doesn't Grandpa come to see us?"

"Because we are Christians."

Jacob's older brother responded in the same way. He did not speak to Jacob at their father's funeral.

Sarah's favorite aunt, Leah, had difficulty with this as well.

How could Sarah do this? Apparently she had forgotten that when one of Sarah's cousins had married a girl of the Christian faith, she and Sarah were among the few relatives who attended the service. The others refused to enter a Christian church.

Sarah thought since Leah had such a strong role in helping those two young people to marry, she would not disapprove of Sarah's conversion.

It was different for Sarah. Leah was upset. Although she did not stop loving Sarah, she hoped the conversion would not be taken too seriously.

Sarah's colleagues at work were equally shaken.

If anyone had thought she converted for business reasons, this was the forum that disproved that idea. Most of her colleagues at the hospital were members of the same Jewish congregation she had joined before she converted. They felt confused when she was not at temple with her family and betrayed when she declared her Christian affiliation.

Was the concept of a Jewish doctor such a novelty in Main Line Philadelphia what it was necessary for her to choose to convert in order to be successful in her profession?

Sarah was perfectly happy being Jewish in that community and that profession. She had the comfort of belonging to a group of neighbors, friends and colleagues which gave her a sense of community and of her roots.

When her inner unrest began, it tore her apart. She never imagined such a thing would happen to her. Her life was completely turned around, converted. That's why she loved the story of Saint Paul's vision on the road to Damascus.

What was he thinking as he walked down the road that day? Was he pondering how Jewish believers could follow that fellow, Jesus, with his open blasphemy of the religion he, Saul, loved?

Was he thinking of how he, a faithful Son of the Covenant could best do God's work by discouraging others from the same wayward path, leading them back to the sheepfold as he understood it?

When Sarah had a discussion about her conversion with one of her most beloved professors who also was Jewish, one whom she admired and respected for his wisdom in life as well as his profession, he made the statement he hoped she would see the error of her ways and "return to the fold."

Was Saint Paul like this man? Saul, a devout and pious Jew was an active persecutor of the followers of The Way because he thought they were going against the God he loved, that they were heretics and blasphemers. He even was involved in the stoning of some of them, Saint Stephen the most famous example. Until that vision of Christ on the read, he was thoroughly convinced he was doing God's will.

What a surprise! The one he was persecuting was God himself. How could he have been so misled? It took three days of blindness before he had recovered enough to ask the question, "What do I do now?"

He was in a situation she understood. Paul was a Jew, an enemy of the church. Although she was not an enemy of the church, she had not been a promoter of it. It was not part of her life. The conversion was not her choice, she repeatedly told members of her family. It came from a higher power, the same one they believed in.

Perhaps if she had not told anyone the situation would have been different.

Did Jairus keep his promise not to tell anyone? The story is recorded in the synoptic Gospels. He must have told someone. Did he wait to tell it later, after Jesus was crucified? Why would he be believed then and not at the time of the event?

Sarah thought it appeared in the Gospels when it made sense to tell about it. Perhaps the world was not ready for the story of that miracle until they were ready to believe miracles can and do occur and God is alive and present in the world.

Sarah's friends and family may not have been ready to hear what she had to say. They had to interpret events in terms they were comfortable with. They knew rational people did not have such experiences. When she would return to her senses, she would understand what she thought had happened didn't happen at all and life would resume its usual rational explainable course.

She was hurt. She would recover. As she developed in her Christian faith, she learned God was indeed a gently loving parent, slow to anger and quick to forgive.

Leaving family to follow Jesus wasn't easy. No one ever said it would be. Things worth doing are often most difficult to do.

What else was there in her life she needed to do? Her explanation was that she was always open to listen to God's voice. When God calls, you must listen.

Chapter 27
The Invasion of the Body

When Sarah retired from performing surgery, she carried many memories of patients and procedures in her heart. As any other craftsman, the surgeon tends to remember certain operations more vividly than others. In Sarah's life there were several such operations.

The first she recalled was the very first one she participated in, the one that made her decide to pursue a career in general surgery. She was a medical student on a surgical rotation. The operation was a vascular procedure designed to bring blood to the lower extremity of a man who had blockages in the arteries to his feet. The patient was anaesthetized by a regional anaesthetic. That meant he was awake and the part to be operated upon was numbed. When the first skin incision was made, Sarah feared she would become ill until she realized the man was not feeling any pain.

Ever since she was a small child, Sarah could not bear to watch any other living thing suffer pain. Knowing the work of surgery could be done without any discomfort convinced her that was the field in which she wanted to practice.

The next operation she recalled vividly was one where the chest of a man was opened and the beating heart was exposed. She was a student on the thoracic service. She was participating in a lung resection under the direction of a thoracic surgeon who shared her reverence for the miracle of the creation of the human body.

How can one describe seeing the living heart beating in the human chest for the first time? She felt great awe for the Creator and such grace for being able to witness this. Could she touch it? It was like touching the center of that person's being. Only one who could appreciate the delicacy and beauty of the human body should be allowed to invade this part of it.

It was after that experience she developed the practice of praying before each operation, thanking God for allowing her to witness the greatness of His work and to ask for His assistance in her work to help heal her patients.

Many years and many operations later, she faced the ultimate test, an event every surgeon dreads. She would have to operate on her own mother. She would not be the primary surgeon, she had a colleague from the next town who would be performing the surgery. She hoped he would call someone else to assist, but he insisted she scrub with him as he trusted her surgical judgment and skill. Reluctantly, she saw his point and agreed to be the assisting surgeon.

Years before Sarah was born, Esther began to suffer with diverticulosis of the colon. When she was a relatively young woman she experienced a hemorrhage from her lower bowel. Her doctor at the time, Dr. Simeone, suggested further investigation and a possible bowel resection. She declined being very much afraid of being in a hospital or of having any surgical procedure. The bleeding stopped spontaneously and did not recur.

Over the ensuing years, she suffered from diverticulitis, but managed to treat this at home without hospitalization.

When Esther was seventy-five, the disease that originated during her younger years caught up with her. She developed severe abdominal pain and fever. She agreed to let Sarah take her to see a doctor this time.

As it is with many children who are physicians, their parents still see them as the little children they raised. Although they proudly tell others of their children's professional accomplishments, they do not trust their medical judgment any more than they would have trusted their ability to make a medical diagnosis as a preschooler.

The doctor Esther saw was a general practitioner, a sweet man who was careful with Esther as she was Sarah's mother. He diagnosed a urinary tract infection but suspected the bowel was the source of the infection. In order to confirm that, he had ordered a barium enema. When Sarah found out what he had done, she was upset. "What if she had a perforation and the barium got into the peritoneal cavity? It would be very difficult to get it out. Why didn't he ask for a study with a water soluble medium?" She reasoned he didn't suspect a perforation, that the urinary tract infection was related to constipation as it often is in the elderly.

Sarah ran down to the X-Ray department to see where the barium had settled. Sure enough, it had pooled outside the bowel. Where was it? No one was certain. Sarah asked for a Foley Catheter to be placed in her mother's urinary bladder and the barium promptly drained out with the urine into the collection bag.

"She has a vesico-colic fistula" she explained to Dr. Langley, her colleague who would be doing the surgery. He lived and worked in a small town twenty-five miles away in rural Georgia.

The diverticulitis had ruptured between Esther's bowel and urinary bladder causing contamination of the urine and a urinary tract infection. It was a common complication of that disease in the elderly, especially ones who do not seek medical treatment until the symptoms are severe. The rupture of the bowel into the bladder is called a vesico-colic fistula.

Dr. Langley came right away to see Esther and insisted Sarah help with the operation. Sarah had hoped to be relieved of being a surgeon that time and hoped she would be treated as the daughter of a patient only.

Her mind was filled with thoughts.

"What if it isn't a fistula, what if she has a tumor or some other potentially fatal condition?"

Sarah sat and thought about it. How could she not go into the operating room? It was her mother who was the patient. How could she sit outside the operating room and wait for Dr. Langley to give her the results of the operation? Her imagination would produce the worst-case scenario regardless of the reality. What difference would it make? What was there was there. Thinking and wishing would not change it. She would have to know sooner or later. Why not be there to see it from the beginning?

She went into the operating room and scrubbed her hands at the sink with Tom Langley.

Esther lay, pale and frail, anaesthetized on the operating table like any other seventy-five year old woman with a vesico-colic fistula. The drainage bag connected to the urinary catheter lay on the floor by the operating table. It was filled with barium from the bladder.

"Let's go!" said Tom as they moved up to the table. He knew her anguish and tried his best to relieve it although his concerns were the same as hers. "What if barium had gotten into the peritoneal cavity? Who in hell had ordered a barium enema?"

Esther's abdomen was draped and the operation began. Tom made the incision where no incision had ever been made before. Esther had never had surgery before in her life.

Sarah knew it would be hard to see this, but she steeled her nerves. This was her mother they were cutting open, the body that housed her before she was born. Her mother was such a modest person she had never let Sarah see her naked. Now she was exposed in a way she had never been before. Her body had been invaded. It was cut open by a man she had met moments before and her own daughter stood opposite him at the operating table and placed her gloved hand into the incision, into the abdominal cavity.

There was the fistula. The bowel was stuck onto the urinary bladder and also to part of the uterus. There was a great deal of inflammation but no sign of spillage of the barium into the peritoneal cavity. There wasn't any stool in the peritoneal cavity either. All they needed to do was to divert the colon and hope for the best, that she would recover and eventually be able to have that portion of the bowel resected, the colon hooked back together at some later date.

Sarah looked at the little uterus, her mother's uterus. It looked like any other belonging to a woman of her age. The ovaries were tiny almond-shaped organs, their surfaces pitted with old scars where ova had once developed and matured. This was the uterus of myth and fable, the one that housed the fetus that would become the baby, Sarah. It was now embedded in the inflammatory mass that was the fistula.

There was no evidence of malignancy. The rest of the abdomen was "unremarkable" as they say.

They brought out a loop of transverse colon onto to abdomen and secured it to the skin. They irrigated the abdomen, closed the incision, dressed it and opened and dressed the colostomy.

"The rest of the abdomen was unremarkable" she thought," except, of course where the patient's daughter had put her hands inside her mother's body and touched the place she had lived before she was born."

Chapter 28
Until the Work is Done

Where do we get the concept that illness is a punishment? Why are we always surprised when a good person becomes ill with a fatal illness while a person who has never done anything good for anyone in his life lives on despite all odds?

Sarah had heard so much of that thinking in support groups, groups of cancer patients and patients with chronic progressive illnesses. She had heard that in meditation groups and prayer groups associated with many churches.

Why were the sick people seen as pariahs? Others would be afraid to care for them fearing their illnesses would be contagious. Suddenly, family members of the dying one would become sugary sweet in their demeanor hoping the "evil eye" would spare them and move on. The disease couldn't even be spoken of in the presence of the dying person; perhaps if we don't mention it, it will go away.

So many times, all the dying person wants to do is talk about the process of dying, to ask questions of doctors, clergy, to give important messages to family members before weakness would overcome them and it would be too late. Often the response would be a denial of the severity of the illness and a flip, "You'll get better, you'll make it through. We are all praying for you."

How could the dying one tell the family he had been praying, too, praying to die peacefully surrounded by loved ones?

When we pray for a person who is dying, what are we asking? Do we ask God to remove the illness therefore proving that God is good? Do we ask the illness be removed to prove that the suffering person is really good and does not deserve to die? Do we ever pray that God will be kind and take that person out of their life peacefully and without further suffering?

Sarah knew there was no such thing as death. She had learned that from her own near-death experience and reports of those of others. She had learned that in church from ministers and from her own explorations into the world of Spirit.

Is there a human being who will not suffer physical death? She was unaware of any or any recorded in history. What is physical death that it was so fearsome it was to be avoided at all cost? Why is the physician the one who feels like a failure whenever a patient dies after all things, ordinary and extraordinary have been done to prolong that patient's life?

Why do we believe that with the proper medical care and the proper spiritual behavior, people will live forever in the human bodies they had since birth?

Sarah's mother died after a long gradual decline. It was a tedious process for both of them. There were frequent times when the possibility of surgery to reverse her colostomy was entertained. Sarah was caught between a rock and a hard place not knowing if Esther would survive another surgery.

Esther had broken a hip several years before her death. It took another year before she was strong enough or cooperative enough to try to walk with a walker. Esther starved herself when she was dissatisfied with the food given to her by Sarah or the nursing home staff where she lived after the hip fracture. The starvation reduced her body protein reserves making healing increasingly difficult. Her paranoia made it impossible to anticipate whether or not she would cooperate with any physician's plan of car. She was suspicious of everyone and resistant to following anyone's suggestions for improving her comfort and health. Nightly, she prayed for God to take her only to wake up to another day.

When a surgeon had her scheduled for surgery to reverse her colostomy, she was excited, anticipating a successful procedure. On the way down the hall from the nursing home to the hospital she was told she would need an intravenous line before the surgery so she might receive antibiotics before the bowel surgery. She refused. The decision was made. Sarah had mixed feelings but it was not her decision as her mother had been declared competent to make her own decisions by hospital psychiatrists. Her mother lived for several more years after that incident and after a long wait, died peacefully in her sleep.

The morning Esther died Sarah was called at home at four AM. That was the time rounds were made in the nursing home and vital signs were taken. Esther appeared to be asleep but was, in fact, dead. Sarah went to the nursing home to do what was required of her and then went home to sleep.

She dreamt her mother was in the morgue, being prepared for embalming. Sarah was there to help prepare the body. She was dressing the colostomy as she had done for years, cleaning the stoma for what would be the final time. For some unknown reason, she could not clean it. Each time she started, there would be a problem either with the material she was using to clean it with, or the dressing wouldn't hold. Esther sat up on the table and started speaking the Sarah.

Sarah was both surprised and pleased. Esther was alive!

"I've just been to the most beautiful place", Esther told her" it was big like the Cathedral of Saint John the Divine. There was heavenly music and huge stained glass windows which made colored patterns on the walls and floors. When I left there I felt well, like I wasn't sick any longer. I feel so well and happy, I can see and hear and move without pain. Do you think since I feel so well we could go to the movies tomorrow?"

That was the end of the dream. Esther asked to go to the movies. How many years had it been since she enjoyed movies with Sarah? It was before her vision and hearing began to fail, before the paranoia became so severe she thought Sarah wanted to harm her. It was a time when Sarah was a student in high school, thirty years before.

Sarah was saddened at Esther's death, but she knew Esther's work had been done. She had lived in that failing body burdened by sensory loss and distorted thinking for so many years. Now she was free. She could enjoy her life in eternity. She felt well. It brought a sense of serenity to Sarah to know that escaping from the prison of that aging body released her immortal spirit to a place where she was again whole and happy.

Chapter 29
The Constant Moon

It was early morning just before dawn, her favorite time of the day. Sarah looked through the screens on the screened porch as she wrote in her journal. On her left she could see the slightest lightening of the sky in the east as the sun sat just below the horizon. To her right, the full moon was high in the sky, producing a silvery glow over the cornfield. The corn tassels were full, like the moon. The tiny ears were ripening, the silks blowing in the gentle breeze. There was corn as far as she could see in the field. Behind the field stood the forest now covered in mist. The mountains beyond were invisible at this hour of the day.

"The moon never changes," she thought "it is the same moon I watched when I was a child in the city."

When she was a child her parents told her there was a man in the moon. She could make out his face. It was the same man in the moon on the cover of the sheet music "Harvest Moon" that sat on Daddy's piano. The man had a pleasant enough face, but where was his body? He watched her as she walked home in the dark after school in the winter. The moon followed her bus as she rode home from night classes. Wherever she went, the man in the moon went with her. Who could predict then he would follow her through time as well?

So many years had passed with the phases of the moon. She had learned so much, lived so long, experienced much sadness and joy in her life and yet the moon had not changed. It was the same moon her father had seen and the same one her grandfather had seen in Europe and on the ship coming to America. It was the same moon that followed the migrations of humans as they set off willingly or not to explore and live in the world. It was the moon astronauts landed upon.

Her Grandma Rivka had lived to see the moon landing. In her very long life she had experienced life before electricity, many wars and then, men landing on the moon.

Sarah thought about her grandparents, how brave they were to leave their homes and villages behind and set off for the New World. How difficult it must have been to learn a new language and a new way of life when one was in one's thirties.

Not so different that what she had done when she followed the voice that led her to Christ.

After she had been a Christian for almost twenty-five years, she began to look back and re-explore her heritage. Her children wanted to know where they came from. No matter where they worshipped, there was a need to catch up with their ethnic identity.

They were invited to the Bar-Mitzvah of a boy who was their friend from school. He had studied hard for that day, having travelled fifty miles each way weekly to go to Hebrew school in another town.

The ceremony seemed endless. It was conducted entirely in Hebrew. Sarah felt as though there was a secret between the boy and the Rabbi that her children were not privileged to know. The boy and friends of his from Hebrew school celebrated this rite of passage with a festive party that was enjoyed by all.

One of Sarah's sons asked if he might have a Bar-Mitzvah.

"Why not", she said, "you have been confirmed in a church. You may do the same in a temple if you want to."

"What were they saying in Hebrew?"

"The same kinds of things they say in English at the confirmation service at church with the exception of the parts about Jesus Christ, of course."

"It's all the same, then?"

"Remember when your older sister took that comparative religion course in college and expressed that idea in class? She asked what the difference was between the Jewish faith and the Christian faith and sorted it out for herself. "So the Jews are waiting for the Messiah to come and the Christians believe he has already come and he is Jesus. That's it? That's the whole thing?"

"Why do people make such a big thing about it?"

"I don't know."

"So we are Jewish and Christian."

"Here we go again" she thought "will it ever end?"

She thought about the moon. It never changed. It reflects the sun's light as long as the sun shines. It has no light of its own. It is a barren rock-like satellite. If the light didn't shine on it, it would not even be visible in the sky.

It's all about light, the light that comes from the Creator. Each one of us has a spark of light as we are told in Kabbalah. Some of us are aware of our own light and the presence of that light in all created beings. We recognize them as part of God's creation and honor them as such. Others feel the need to separate from that light so they put up shields and insulate themselves from the Glory that is God. Regardless, we are dependent upon the source, not upon ourselves for that light. Without our source of light we are like the moon, a barren rock.

The face of the man in the moon exists because the light of the sun shines on it. It is no more a face than we are self-created. We receive the spark from God. Whatever we do, whatever we believe, it is God who holds the light. The light is the love of the Creator for the creation. It is the Light of the World. It is the Light of Christ.

www.ingramcontent.com/pod-product-compliance
Lightning Source LLC
Chambersburg PA
CBHW052133170626
46812CB00004B/1394